HENRI MARTIN

ISUREN
AND OTHER STORIES

TRANSLATED AND WITH AN INTRODUCTION BY
BRIAN STABLEFORD

THIS IS A SNUGGLY BOOK

Translations and Introduction
Copyright © 2023 by Brian Stableford.
All rights reserved.

ISBN: 978-1-64525-127-9

ISUREN
AND OTHER STORIES

HENRI MARTIN (1810-1883) was born in Saint-Quentin in the Aisne. After moving to Paris, he joined Charles Nodier's cénacle and made the acquaintance of many of the leading figures of the Romantic Movement. Though mostly remembered today as a historian, due to his *Histoire de France*, a massive work in 13 volumes (1833-1836), he also wrote fiction of note, including the long historical melodrama, *Wolfthurm, ou Le Tour du loup* (1830), which was produced with his friend Félix Davin, and the story "Isuren," the first significant French contribution to what eventually became a subgenre of "prehistoric fantasy."

BRIAN STABLEFORD's scholarly work includes *The Plurality of Imaginary Worlds: The Evolution of French roman scientifique* (Black Coat Press, 2017) and *Tales of Enchantment and Disenchantment: A History of Faerie* (Black Coat Press, 2019). He has translated more than three hundred volumes from the French, mostly in the genres of *roman scientifique* and Romantic and Symbolist fiction. His recent fiction includes the visionary science fiction novel *The Revelations of Time and Space* (2020) and its sequel *After the Revelation* (2021); the last in his long series of "Tales of the Genetic Revolution," *The Elusive Shadows* (2020); and the comedy fantasy *Meat on the Bone* (2021), all published by Snuggly Books.

CONTENTS

INTRODUCTION

HENRI MARTIN (1810-1883) was born in Saint-Quentin in the Aisne, and formed a friendship there in his youth with the slightly older Félix Davin (1807-1836). Both had literary ambitions and they collaborated on a long historical melodrama, *Wolfthurm, ou Le Tour du loup*,[1] published in two volumes in 1830. In Paris they joined Charles Nodier's cénacle and made the acquaintance of many of the leading figures of the Romantic Movement. The prolific Davin was immediately successful, joining the staff of the satirical weekly *Le Figaro*, alongside other members of the Movement, and publishing several novels before dying prematurely of tuberculosis.

---

1 *Wolfthurm* was by-lined "Félix et Iner"; some modern biographies and the most recent print-on-demand reprint represent Davin as the sole author, but that is incorrect.

Davin and Martin both appear to have been linked with the coterie surrounding Honoré de Balzac and his close friend Samuel-Henri Berthoud, who signed his work "S. Henry Berthoud," and Martin also became closely associated with "P. L. Jacob le bibliophile" (Paul Lacroix), with whom he undertook to compile a historical work initially planned as a kind of anthology, collecting excerpts from chronicles and other existing texts. Martin swiftly became the more determined and more adventurous contributor to the collaboration, however, which formed the launching-pad for his ambitious popular *Histoire de France depuis les temps les plus reculés jusqu'en juillet 1830*, the first volume of which was issued in 1833 and the thirteenth in 1836. He continued to expand it, until it occupied nineteen volumes in 1865, and was augmented thereafter by several detailed supplements, including a six-volume *Histoire de France depuis 1789 juqu'à nos jours* (1879-83). A popular abridgement of the earlier text had earlier been published in seven volumes in 1877, by which time Martin had embarked on a political career, initially serving as a député for the Aisne.

Although his endeavor was outshone by the equally voluminous history that had been published more than a decade before by his fellow Romantic historian Jules Michelet (1798-1874), Martin was elected to the Académie française in 1878, an appointment probably not unconnected with his status as a recently-appointed senator and his presidency of the Ligue de Patriotes. By then he was firmly associated with the idea of "Romantic nationalism," whereas Michelet was primarily reputed for his fervent republican views, which had not been well received during the Second Empire. Under the so-called Third Republic, although it was regarded as a fake by many neo-Romantics who never forgave its leaders for the brutality with which they had put down the Paris Commune in 1870 and punished its leaders, Martin and Michelet both reinforced their heroic status, but the reputation of the latter held up better in the assessment of the political left. Although both were inventive narrative historians never inclined to let mere facts get in the way of telling the kind of story they wanted to construct, the particular improvisations made by Martin fared worse in the face of criticism by more accurate analysts; he had lent very heavy emphasis in the opening volume of his history to an "origin myth" that anchored French history and national identity in the exploits and conquests of "Gauls" in the centuries before the Roman invasions of the territory that eventually became France, and its consequent Christianization.

A substantial contribution to the improvisations made by Martin in constructing that origin myth were made by another of the friends he made within the Romantic Movement of the early 1930s, Jean Reynaud (1806-1863), a devout follower of the utopian and religious philosophies of the Comte de Saint-Simon. Reynaud was one of the directors of and principal contributors to the *Encyclopédie nouvelle* of 1836, and he made significant contributions to geological science before combining his various ideas in a remarkable text entitled *Terre et Ciel* (1854), categorized on its title page as "philosophie religieuse." The book presents an evolutionary history of the earth from its cosmic origins through the emergence of human beings and the "origin of the soul," and then replaces the soul in a cosmic context that includes angels as well as planetary beings, in which humans, like all other living beings, are subject to a gradual evolution toward spiritual perfection, facilitated by serial reincarnation. The book became one of the key texts of the French "Occult Revival," not least because Reynaud and Martin had attributed a primitive version of that religious philosophy to "druids" who were, in their imagination, the spiritual leaders of the Gauls, and hence of a primitive culture overlaid but not quite exterminated by the Christianity forcibly imposed on Western Europe by Roman legions.

While teaming up with the Bibliophile Jacob and devoting himself to the study and construction of history, Martin also made several contributions to *L'Artiste*, one of the most successful of a group of new Romantic periodicals founded in the wake of the July Revolution of 1830, which had put an end to the "absolutist" Bourbon monarchy and replaced it with the "constitutional" monarchy of Louis-Philippe. Prior to that date, political censorship of periodicals had been extremely severe, and Romantic publications, which were rightly suspected of Republican sympathies, were subject to forceful suppression. The few that were able to continue publication—most significantly the *Mercure du XIXe siècle*, which enjoyed a precarious existence between 1823 and 1830—did so by representing themselves as purely artistic and literary in their interests. *L'Artiste* continued that policy, devoting its core content to accounts of the annual Salon, and publishing engravings of many of the art works exhibited there. It also published literary criticism and fiction, however, and to begin with, the material it used was much less staid than the academic art featured in its illustrations. It continued a strategy employed by the *Mercure* of featuring work translated from German and English, often fantastic in nature, but it also published work by a few French Romantics, probably deliberately testing the tolerance of the new regime—whose censors soon proved to be only marginally less oppressive than those of the Bourbon era.

One of the contributors of original fiction to *L'Artiste* in 1831-2 was the outspoken arch-radical Félix Pyat, later to be one of the prime movers of the Commune, who famously became involved in a fierce dispute with another contributor, Jules Janin. From the viewpoint of today, their contributions to the periodical seem inoffensive, but at the time the publication of their work was potentially hazardous, and *L'Artiste*'s editors were well aware of the risks they were taking. After 1832 the editorial policy changed markedly, and the fiction featured in the periodical became much more anodyne. Several of the authors who had contributed to it in its first two years vanished from its pages, including Félix Pyat and Henri Martin. The disappearance of Martin's work might have surprised readers slightly at the time, but those readers would not have known that in addition to the five stories carrying his by-line, Martin had contributed a sixth item, which had not carried a signature, the content of which was bound to be controversial and to stir up trouble.

The story in question was reprinted twice in later decades, with Martin's by-line included, so there is no doubt as to its authorship, but it is not entirely surprising that the author and the editors thought it diplomatic not to attach a signature to the first printing, and the omission might have been wise. The story in question was "Isuren, histoire tirée des annals de Kachmyr," and the author and editors must have known that it would call forth an angry and hostile reaction from a sector of their audience whose sensitivity and influence was notorious: the devout. "Isuren" was the first significant French contribution to what eventually became a subgenre of "prehistoric fantasy," extensively developed in the *belle époque*, when the censorious privileges of the Church had finally evaporated, by such neo-Romantic writers as J. H. Rosny and Edmond Haraucourt.

"Isuren" offers a fictional account of the emergence of the human race in the course of the geological evolution of the planet, and it represents that emergence explicitly as an initial "evolution of the soul." Although it deliberately employs symbolism appropriated from the Old Testament—including the deluge and the burning bush—it does so ironically, in order to provide a hypothetical sociopsychological account of the origin of religion. It does not deny the existence of God—indeed, it supports that notion—but the God it admits and celebrates is "the god of the philosophers," a far remoter figure than the God of the Scriptures, whose only role in the story's backcloth is that of an imaginative fiction requiring historical explanation. The story was thus bound to cause offense to the Churchmen of France in 1832, and presumably did; it might well have been protests that they made behind the scenes that prompted the subsequent change in *L'Artiste*'s editorial policy.

Although that interference left no explicit evidence, it is worth bearing in mind the history of two other prehistoric fantasies that were published in relatively quick succession after "Isuren" in other Romantic periodicals founded during the burst of optimism that succeeded the July Revolution is 1830. The first was the opening section of a novella entitled "Histoire d'une civilisation antédiluvienne" published in the *Revue de Paris* a few months later in 1832, which bore the signature "Jonathan le visionnaire"; the character in question had previously featured as the notional narrator of a series of stories published in the *Mercure du XIXe siècle* in the early 1920s, whose author usually used the signature "X. B. Saintine" (Joseph-Xavier Boniface). That series had been reprinted in book form as *Jonathan le visionnaire* (1823; revised edition 1825 as *Les Soirées de Jonathan*), but when the revised collection was reprinted again in 1936, the novella was not added, nor was it included in a further version issued in 1853, although it was supplemented in an edition published after the author's death in 1866 (it is included in the translation published as *Jonathan the Visionary* in 2018).

The third prehistoric fantasy of the period, which was even more daring in representing the prehistoric ancestors of *Homo sapiens* as ape-like creatures, was the second part of "Paris avant les hommes" by the naturalist Pierre Boitard, a paleontological study included in volume V of the didactic *Musée des familles* (1834). It was published there after Boitard's death by his close friend, the editor of the *Musée*, Samuel-Henri Berthoud, who had previously been the last editor of the *Mercure* prior to its abrupt closure, and who was sacked as editor of the *Musée* shortly after publishing the Boitard story, as a result of the outcry it provoked. Berthoud was probably the uncredited editor of the *Journal des Femmes* when it reprinted "Isuren" in its February 1844 issue, as "Le Feu," with Martin's signature attached, and he might also have had some involvement in assembling the anthology *Les Plumes d'or*, published by Dentu on behalf of the Societé des gens de letters, in 1865, where it was reprinted again under its original title. Berthoud made his own pioneering contribution to the genre in "Les Premier habitants de Paris," the first part of *L'Homme depuis cinq mille ans* (1865). That date is primarily significant in demonstrating that it took Berthoud some thirty years to publish a story in the genre, which he would surely have done in the early 1830s had it been practicable. Martin, like Saintine, published nothing else similar in his lifetime, just as Boitard had not. Publishing "Isuren" was, therefore, a bold move in 1832—bolder, on the part of the editors of *L'Artiste*, than publishing the items by Félix Pyat that appeared alongside it.[1]

---

1 The biography of Berthoud included in J. M. Quérard's *La Littérature français contemporaine* (1842),

The other stories that Martin contributed to *L'Artiste*, which appeared there in the same order in which their translations appear in the present collection, the last of them in 1833, are much more conventional, and might be reckoned typical products of the Romantic Movement at that point in its evolution, when Balzac, Berthoud and Petrus Borel were all engaged in the discussions of narrative strategy and propriety that helped formulate the subgenre that Berthoud called *Contes misanthropiques* (1831) and Borel "*contes immoraux*" (in the subtitle of *Champavert*, 1833) but which later came to be known as *contes cruels*. Although only one of Martin's stories—"Le Wivre," tr. as "The Wyvern"[1]—really qualifies

obviously supplied by the author, lists *L'Artiste* as one of the periodicals to which he had lent editorial assistance; as the son of a printer who was experienced in the technical procedure of putting together issues of periodicals he was recruited to help with many of the new periodicals founded in the post-1830 boom. It is not impossible, therefore, that he had some influence on the decision to publish "Isuren." Martin shared Berthoud's strong interest in the legends and folklore of northern France, and it might have been Berthoud's example that led him sometimes to adapt his own signature to "Henry Martin" during the early years of his career.

1 The first part of "Le Wivre" had previously appeared, anonymously, in Emile Girardin's fashion magazine *La Mode*—another periodical in whose production and

as a fully-fledged *conte cruel*, and one—"Le
Marchand de Cairo," tr. as "The Merchant of
Cairo"—deliberately ducks out of being one
by evoking one of the standard clichés used
for blunting climactic cruelty, the fact that
such discussions were ongoing at the time of
their composition is surely not irrelevant to
their tone and narrative trajectories.

"Le Marchand de Cairo" was presumably
written in full awareness of and wry reaction to devout criticism of "Isuren," and its
subtle rhetoric is convoluted. Superficially
a flamboyant denial of atheism, it is surely
an ironic exercise in deliberate insincerity.
It contrasts sharply with "Une Aventure de
l'Abbé de Gondy" (tr. as "An Adventure of
the Abbé de Gondy") the naturalistic fantasy
of recent history that followed it, and equally
sharply with, "La Fille du jarl" (tr. as "The
Jarl's Daughter"), a straightforward exercise
in pastiche reflecting the recent interest of
the French Romantics in Scandinavian liter-
ature, which fit in well enough with *L'Artiste*'s
changed editorial policy. What the latter two
stories have in common, in spite of their

---

editing Samuel-Henri Berthoud assisted—in 1831,
but the remainder of the story, advertised as to be
continued in the next issue, did not appear there; no
explanation was given.

18

contrast in setting and style, is a skeptical attitude to religion; in the former story the institutions of the Catholic Church are employed hypocritically as an agent of wicked tyranny; in the latter parable, mutual religious intolerance is brutally and fatally destructive. Various as they are, the three stories that followed "Isuren" in the pages of *L'Artiste* all bear the scars of the reaction against it.

The first of the five stories published there in 1832—although it was presumably written after "Le Wivre"—"Le Mauvais oeil" (tr. as "The Evil Eye") transplants an item of European folklore, most famously adapted into Romantic fiction by Théophile Gautier in the similarly tragic "Jettatura" (1856),[1] into an Oriental setting. "Le Wivre" scorns that conventional distancing move but makes a much more adventurous and similarly-prompted attempt at originality in its innovative characterization of its Satanic villain—a stratagem employed by several of

----

1 As an interesting aside, "Une Nuit," signed E. Brac de Bourdonnel, another story featured in *L'Artiste* in 1832, immediately before Martin's "Le Mauvais oeil," is a synopsis of the anecdote featured in one of Gautier's most famous stories, "Une Nuit de Cléopâtre" (1838), but the named author was real and the appropriation appears to have been Gautier's; it is not unlikely that Gautier read and remembered "Le Mauvais oeil."

Martin's contemporaries, including Alphonse Brot, who became a successful specialist in historical fiction, in his remarkable surreal transformation of "Faust" (1833). Although "Le Marchand de Cairo" settles for a more conventional ending, the build-up to its climax embodies a similar proto-surrealism, also found in the opium-influenced fantasies of Charles Nodier, Théophile Gautier and Alphonse Karr. There is thus a thread of continuity running through all six of Martin's stories in terms of their Romantic enterprise.

"Une Aventure de l'Abbé de Gondy" is much more closely related than its predecessors to the kind of historical speculation that was to occupy Martin for the rest of his career. The first volume of his *Histoire de France*, published in 1833, is almost entirely a work of eccentric speculative fiction, a very obvious scholarly fantasy, and although the later volumes are much less obviously fantasized, it is worth remembering that all Romantic history involves the strategic employment of the imagination, in that the historian routinely attempts to "place himself in the shoes" of historical actors in order to deduce their motivation and sentiments. In his formal history, Martin did not dare to hypothesize that the puzzling features of the remarkable career of

Cardinal de Retz might be explicable in terms of an event like the one imagined in the story, but it is easy to see how a Romantic historian studying the known facts of the cardinal's life and his self-serving memoirs might have ventured some such psychological hypothesis. More than one of Martin's friends—most obviously Alphonse Brot and Félix Davin—made careers out of the fictional representation of such imaginative endeavors, and the line separating their exercises in admitted invention from the scholarly endeavors of Martin and Michelet is thinner than it pretends to be.

The present volume is a relatively meager one—it is not entirely surprising that no such volume was ever compiled in France, and that Martin left it to others to preserve "Isuren" in slightly more durable form than its original appearance—but it is nevertheless a volume that shows considerable enterprise and originality, in more ways than one. The legacy of the fiction of the Romantic Movement was stifled even during the reign of Louis-Philippe before being virtually exterminated in the first decade of the Second Empire, and never received the attention it deserved from subsequent historians. Martin's contribution to the boom that followed the July Revolution was brief, and, like so many others, he gave up in despair of being able to find and maintain an audience, eventually finding an alternative route to success and the Académie, but his fiction does not deserve to be forgotten, and still has much to offer modern readers, especially to connoisseurs of fantastic fiction.

—Brian Stableford

ISUREN
AND OTHER STORIES

THE EVIL EYE
A Tale of the Kahveh Khaneh[1]

There is no shield that resists your eyes
—Asdjedy[2]

THE first fires of dawn were blanching the citadel of Gamdan on the high hill, and causing to spring forth luminously from the obscure masses of the great Sana the square towers of minarets and the large domes of mosques, when several litters borne by slaves emerged from the labyrinth of gardens that surrounded the royal city like an immense flower-bed. Traversing the delightful valley of

---

1 Author's note: "Kahveh Khaneh: literally, coffee house. It is normally in coffee houses that Oriental storytellers make their stories heard."
2 Asdjedy, or Asdjedi, was a poet of the tenth-century "Persian renaissance," contemporary with Ferdoussi, or Firdausi.

Rodda, they headed toward the mountainous region of the Djiabal.

Oh, no man who parted the pink silk curtains of the first litter would have traded what they hid for all the treasures of Ima in Yemen.

He might have seen, floating over a neck whiter than a jasmine flower, tresses as black as musk; he might have seen, leaning over a small and delicate hand, a gracious forehead of fifteen years, and two lowered eyes veiled by long lashes, which raised their elongated almonds with azure irises toward him. If a smile had suddenly appeared between those pursed and pensive lips, pearls more precious than the pearls of Bahrein enlaced in the young woman's braided hair, doubtless the indiscreet stranger's reason would have fled with his heart; he would have sworn to possess Leila or to die!

But the virgin's gaze was not lifted; her lips did not part in order to smile, and the gleam of tulips disappeared from her cheeks before the pallor of lilies.

Whence comes that melancholy, then, under which the charming head of the daughter of the Emir Farhan is bowed, who had once frolicked through life, as insouciant and light as a gazelle of the Nedjed? Her past was all joy and innocence; her future . . .

In the mountains and in the plain, from the shores of Aden to the rocks of Khaulan, there was no daughter of a sheikh or emir who did not envy the fiancée of the rich, powerful and handsome Mansor, the proud dola of Sanhan! She had seemed to receive her father's orders with a satisfied soul, and more than once she had followed with an attentive gaze the dola's long-maned mare when he passed at a gallop before her jealousy.

However, this is not the sweet reverie of a fiancée who trembles with emotion and hope at the moment of crossing the threshold of an unknown world; there is suffering in that languor, anxiety and a kind of somber presentiment in that mild physiognomy. For an entire month she has not been behind her loophole to watch the dola and his brilliant escort pass by, and a kind of fear contracts her features when her father talks to her about the approaching marriage.

She has been thus since a stranger has seen her face at the hour of morning prayer.

One day, when she was walking on the balcony of her father's palace, shortly after the muezzin had summoned the faithful to the first prayer, she chanced to lift her head toward a minaret adjacent to the corner of the terrace where she was walking. The muezzin was no longer there, but in his place a hadji was standing, leaning on the balustrade of the tower. At first Leila wanted to withdraw, frightened by seeing a stranger at that dominant point, to which only blind muezzins have the right to climb. An irresistible force retained her; in any case, the stranger did not seem to perceive her presence. He was tall and slim; his face, which she could only see in profile, was handsome and sad, like that of a Peri thinking about the Eden from which his race was exiled. One might have thought that the iron fingers of fatality had furrowed that noble and as-yet-young physiognomy with profound traces, thinning its angular contours by tightening them.

Leila was gazing at him with an indefinable constriction of the heart when he suddenly turned sideways and lowered upon her two large dark eyes, profoundly sunk in their orbits, which emitted a strange and somber flame like the cavities of a double crater. It seemed to her that the rays of the hadji's gaze had penetrated her breast like two burning arrows; a sensation that was both an unspeakable dolor and a delirious pleasure caused her entire being to shudder; everything vacillated around her and she fell against a trellis, palpitating and almost fainting. But although all the other objects were floating confusedly in her gaze, she could still see the stranger distinctly. He leaned toward her, hiding his forehead in his hands; then he straightened up, made a movement to return to the interior of the minaret, stopped momentarily, darted an oblique glance at the young woman—and, striking his breast with a gesture of despair, he disappeared into the stairway.

That is what has caused Leila's melancholy.

And this morning, she is more absorbed than ever in her thoughts; for she knows that she is returning as a virgin for the last time to her father's country house, and that she will only see the royal city again on her bridal camel. So she is gazing indifferently at the fresh hills covered with rich plantations of coffee-trees, the elegant groups of date-palms with large fans, and the sand dunes where trees of Judea make their pink bouquets shine amid the foliage of the cheerful acacias: gracious landscapes that she once loved to see passing by turns alongside her litter.

Silence! Who is brushing the branches of the balm-trees thus? Are those brown heads that are parting the leaves the malicious faces of apes that have come to grimace at the travelers? The slaves have stopped; the eunuchs are whispering and putting their hands on their sabers. Disaster! A troop of men with grim faces launch forth from the bushes, muskets in hand. Their black hair, circled by a simple cord, and their muscular bodies, naked save for a loincloth, make them recognizable as Kobaïls from the mountains of the North. Disaster!—for pillage, devastation and death are the companions of the Kobaïl.

A cry of distress rises in the little caravan; a discharge thunders, and three eunuchs fall under the devastating bullets of the muskets. The slaves flee; Leila's women throw themselves out of their litters and disperse. Abandoned by all those who surrounded her, the daughter of Farhan invokes the Lord and his prophet in the depths of her heart and flees like a young antelope surprised by a cruel panther.

Alas, the avid eyes of the marauders have seen the pearls shining in her hair and the gold of her rich necklace; they all run after her. Their rapid surge devours the distance that separates her from them; their iron leg-muscles will soon have wearied the frail and gracious legs of a young woman accustomed to the slack idleness of the harem. Exhausted, breathless, she feels her knees buckling beneath her; she gets up again to resume her course, totters and collapses on the burning soil.

She sees the Kobaïls arriving, without being able to make an effort to escape the fate that threatens her. Horrible! A horrible moment! Here they come, here they come! They are bounding and howling, already extending their arms, tensed by impatience and rapacity.

At that moment, a man clad in the long white garment of a hadji emerges from a clump of palms and places himself between the mountain men and the daughter of Farhan.

An electric flame ran through Leila's veins; she had not seen his face, which was turned toward the Kobaïls, but she understood well enough that it was him!

He was wearing a trenchant dagger in his belt but he did not draw it. Leila saw him fold his arms and stand still, only imprinting a slight movement on his head, as if he were looking at all the marauders one after another.

The latter stopped in mid-leap; their fixed gazes were suspended on that of the stranger; the passions that swelled the muscles of their faces had given way to a bleak stupefaction. Then the hadji raised his right arm and extended his index finger toward a clump of coffee bushes that rose up some distance away. The brigands gripped their scimitars angrily, grinding their teeth; their breasts swelled, and they appeared to be making a violent effort to tear themselves away from the unknown force that was nailing them to the spot, in order to hurl themselves forward; but the hadji's finger made a more imperious gesture, and they recoiled slowly, following the direction that he imposed on them, and finally disappeared into the coffee-trees.

Then he turned toward the woman he had just saved. She got to her feet; not knowing what she was doing, and, incapable of sustaining herself, she let her head fall on the shoulder of her liberator. He shivered; his eyes were shining like those of a lioness who has just fought for her cubs; but their gleam was as sharp and as penetrating as on the day when it had been fixed on Leila for the first time. Leila felt her heart pierced by a strange pain—but she would have given her entire life for that instant; she would have died without a plaint!

Suddenly, the stranger uttered a dull groan, and pulled the hood of his ample marlotte over his face.

"Daughter of Farhan," he said, in a low and compressed voice, "I shall take you back to your father."

Leila did not reply, but she covered her head with her almizar, and they set forth silently.

They went for a long time in that manner; the hadji's bosom rose convulsively, but his

tongue was mute and his head was bowed—
and yet, if he had looked at the woman who
was walking behind him meekly he might
have discovered treasures of joy in the blue
eyes that were shining behind the transparent
gauze of the almizar.

A delightful scenery was deployed around
them; a light breeze was refreshing the burning atmosphere and murmuring melodiously
in the branches, carrying through the air the
multiple perfumes of myrrh, jasmine, incense,
cinnamon and coffee; a thousand birds were
singing, hopping and fluttering among the
verdant masses of foliage, the red clusters of
the date-palms and the white flowers of the
mimosas. Everything was sighing, embalming
the air and undulating vaguely, bearing upon
the heart.

The hadji finally spoke, and his voice was
sweeter than the sound of the vina, sadder
than the song of a bird of paradise at the moment when it expires.

"Do you understand, young woman, the
embalmed breeze that is agitating your veil as
it passes? It is the amorous breath of nature,
which warms and perfumes the nuptial bed of
all creatures. Look: green snakes are enlacing
their flexible coils and embracing gently under
the branches of thee acacias; turtle-doves are

moaning in an excess of happiness, intoxicat-
ed by endless kisses; red grouse are calling to
one another breathlessly under the cinnamon
trees. Everything loves, everything unites under the sky, without fear and without remorse!
I alone am rejected by that concert of amour
and harmony; for me alone to love is a crime."

"Why?" said Lela, naively.

"Why?" repeated the stranger—and his tone
became hoarse, as lugubrious as a death-rattle.
"Don't ask me that, young woman. For pity's
sake, don't ask me that. You are here, beside
me, confident and tranquil, like a little bird
under its mother's wing. Do you want to flee
me, then, with more horror than a squirrel of
the palm trees flees the murderous gaze of a
snake?"

"I won't flee!" she said, in a voice that was
simultaneously firm and infantile.

He threw himself at the young woman's
feet with a stifled cry and embraced her knees
forcefully. Then, getting to his feet, he said,
impetuously: "Oh, don't speak to me in that
soft voice, don't say such things to me, for the
frightful sacrifice would become impossible
for me—and yet, it's necessary, it's imperative
that I quit you forever, that I submit to my
destiny alone, that I save you from me!"

A second *why* expired on Leila's lips.

At that moment, cries became audible; they were calling "Leila! Leila!" and several men, yataghans in hand, ran toward the young woman. They were Emir Farhan and his man, who had learned from fugitive slaves about the attack on the escort and had come running to rescue the young woman they supposed to be a captive of the mountain-dwellers. They gazed with astonishment at the hadji.

The latter advanced toward the old chief.

"Emir Farhan," he said, "here is your daughter, whom I have saved from the hands of the Kobaïls; I replace her in yours, pure."

"Peace be with you!" cried the old man. "May the blessings of the prophet accompany you, O faithful Muslim! Would you like my most beautiful mare and the lightest of my dromedaries? Would you like half my hills, green with odorous coffee bushes, and my most beautiful garden in the valley of Rodda, with its rose- and lilac-bushes and its jasmine arbors? All that is yours, if you wish, O saintly hadji, who has returned my unique child to me!"

"I am not a saint before the Lord," replied the stranger, in a grave and somber tone. "May Allah recompense you for your generous offers, but I cannot accept them; I have no use for the wealth of this world."

And he drew away slowly, leaving in the souls of Farhan and his men a singular impression of respect and dread. For Leila, when she no longer saw his blue mantle between the trees and could no longer hear the sound of his footfalls, it seemed that a mortal silence had succeeded the countless harmonies that had filled her heart a moment before, and that a dull and colorless veil extended over all of nature.

The days went by, and with them Leila's sadness augmented. Her eyes, often moist, shone in her sweet face like violets in a field of snow. She begged her father to withdraw the promise that he had given to Mansor, but the emir's brow became severe, and he asked whether she wanted him to break his word, like a kafir who does not believe in God, and he ordered her to prepare to be the wife of the dola, who was already her husband in the eyes of the law—for he had seen her without her veil—the following day.

The emir did not know that he was not the only one!

Leila withdrew, pale and unsteady. She plunged into the darkest shade in the garden, and wept.

She heard a rustle in the bushes, and a man dressed as a slave came to prostrate himself before her. A slight blush colored Leila's features; a smile parted her lips momentarily—but only momentarily, for it was immediately succeeded by a movement of alarm.

"Oh," murmured the stranger, "forgive me! I wanted to see you again one more time before going away forever. No, don't look at me! No, but let me hear your voice! A word, a single word, and then I'll go, and you can expel from your memory this lugubrious apparition, which will have disappeared before becoming fatal to you—but speak to me once more! Oh, you're trembling, I see; it's your good angel that is warning you. It is right; but I shall not engage you to close your ears."

"Adjem,"[1] said the young woman, in a hesitant voice, "if I'm afraid, it's for you! Alas, if they catch you here, they'll cut off your head with their yataghans, without my being able to defend you. Go away! The idea of your danger is causing me to die in advance!"

---

1 Presumably the author's rendering of the Arabic word more usually given as *ajam*, in this instance meaning "Be quiet!"

"I would have liked to finish thus," he replied, "but since you do not wish it, be tranquil; I have nothing to fear from men. The savage Kobaïls are not the only enemies that I am able to tame!" And his smile was as proud, as ironic and as sad as that of a rebel djinni. "Alas," he went on, "I'm accursed for having sought to trouble your life again, but I don't have the strength to resist. Pardon me—I love you so much!"

"I love you too," she said, placing her little hand on the stranger's shoulder.

He threw himself on that hand, which he covered with kisses and burning tears.

"Oh, woe betide you, daughter of Yemen! For pity's sake, don't pronounce that word!"

"I love you," she repeated, "but the other is marrying me tomorrow!"

The hadji leapt backwards, like a tiger; then his head slumped upon his breast.

"Marry him," he said, in a dull voice, "marry him, and send me away, for my love is a gift of Hell!"

"Yes, I want you to leave here—but you won't depart alone. Who would wipe the dust of the journey from your brow then? Who would veil your face when you sleep in the sun? Adjem; you must take me with you tomorrow."

"Do you know to whom you want to deliver yourself, poor imprudent gazelle throwing yourself foolishly into the lion's mouth? Do you know the wretch who is before you? Listen . . ."

"It's futile! It's too late. Your first gaze engraved you in my heart in ineffaceable traces. The sight of you pleases and lacerates me, plunges me into a bleak abatement and then enraptures me with ineffable transports. I don't know whether you will be deadly to me, as you say, but it's necessary that I go with you, for it is written!"

"Are you weary of living, then, young woman? So much youth and beauty sacrificed to one accursed, like me? No! I cannot!"

She took a short, light stiletto from her belt, a frail and delicate ornament that could have shone in her hair if necessary, like a great golden needle with a head of turquoise and onyx.

"Do you believe that a woman's hand can weigh enough upon this blade to make it reach her heart? You will abduct me tomorrow, or this dagger will have touched me before Mansor. Do you not have a mare as rapid as a mountain eagle?"

"Yes."

"Well, be ready with it near this garden; sound a trumpet to warn me of your arrival. In the midst of the tumult of the celebration, when my companions prepare to place me on the bridal camel to take me to Sana, I'll escape from the nuptial cortege; I'll flee through the gardens, which won't be guarded, and I'll be yours! No response: go quickly, for the eunuchs are about to make their evening round. Adieu! Until tomorrow!"

She had disappeared.

The hadji pressed his breast forcefully with both hands.

"Yes, it was written!" he said.

The next day, at dawn, numerous horsemen arrived at the country house of Emir Farhan Nothing could be seen in the distance along the road but the sheiks of Téhama clad in long abas as white as camphor, djiabalys in broad striped chemises, magnificent caftans, and large turbans of undulating muslin. There was a continuous file of horses, camels and litters, between the curtains of which heads veiled by embroidered almizars appeared.

All her companions are clustered around the beautiful bride. They have already brought her from the bath; they have ornamented her neck with brilliant golden chains, and her head with a rich turban, from which bandlets of silver gauze are suspended; they attach balls of ruby and opal to her ears and pass gold circlets around her slender arms and legs; they paint her nails with carmine and henna, blacken her eyelids with powered kohl and perfume her beautiful hair with benzoin and civette. She allows them to decorate her like the marble statue of some divinity, less white and less cold than her. All of her blood has flowed back to her heart; but if some slight noise rises up—the cry of a samarmog perched in the branches of a sycamore, the whinny of a mare, or the whistle of a camel-driver summoning his dromedaries—she shivers and her pale cheeks are suddenly inflamed by a red tint, like clouds at sunset.

She listened in vain; the trumpet had not projected its clear and prolonged voice through the noise of the fête. She went up to the high terrace and gazed into the distance, with a gaze as piercing as that of a swallow searching for her stolen chicks; but the vale was silent and deserted; nothing whitened in the sunlight between the nopals and the fig-trees.

Then she slipped her dagger, which she had hidden in a jasmine, into her bosom and went down toward her companions, who led her away, mute and docile, into the courtyard, where a camel was waiting, caparisoned with bright carpets, its head ornamented with floating ostrich plumes. Its neck enlaced by garlands of flowers. The bride was seated on the camel and the joyful caravan set forth for Sana to the song of hautboys, tambours and cymbals.

Leila took once again, with her cortege, the route that she had traveled with another company. She saw again the hills covered with coffee-trees and the boscage were the birds were singing amorously; and when she passed close to the palm trees from which he had emerged in order to save her from the Kobaïls, a bitter regret seized her heart.

Why had it happened? Everything would be finished now! The noisy marriage feast would be celebrated in the emir's palace, and when evening came, after the young women had danced to the tambours and sung the praises of the bride, after everyone had begged Allah and his prophet Mohammed to bless the union of Mansor and Leila, to give their sons the courage of Antar and the wealth of Karoun, and their daughters the beauty and virtue of Aïesha, and to preserve the two spouses from the evil spells of enchanters and the gaze of the evil eye, the assembly would conduct the married couple to the nuptial chamber and leave them alone there.

The men would wait for a long time in the banqueting hall for the husband to come to announce his victory to the relatives and friends; the women would wait in the harem for the young bride to come and join them, confused and blushing, to pass the rest of the mysterious night among them.

No one appeared; they listened; a mortal silence reigned in the spouses' apartment. They called out, but obtained no response.

Anxiety took hold of all the witnesses; superstitious terrors agitated minds. People ran to fetch the father of the bride, who, in accordance with custom, had drawn away during the supreme hour of his daughter's virginity. He seized a cornelian consecrated by the talismanic names of protective angels and, opening the curtains that separated the fatal chamber from the next room, he hurled himself into it, his heart constricted by suspense and anguish.

By the red radiance of the torch he saw the bed, empty and in order. A little further away, a confused mass lay on the floor. He approached; it was the dola Mansor.

Leila had disappeared,

Farhan cried out; everyone cane running; Mansor was lifted up. He was only unconscious and bore no trace of any wound.

When he came round, nothing could be obtained from him but vague and incoherent words, imprinted with a profound terror; his reason had departed forever.

The moon is asleep over the great desert of Djilof.

Under a solitary dune that rises in the plain, the rim of a somber cavern opens; one of Phingary's rays slides through the nopal and basilics that block the mouth of the lair and extends far enough into the depths to repose upon two immobile but living objects. Is that a lion lying on dry palm leaves with his royal companion? No, it is a pilgrim of Mecca who is hiding his face under the folds of his marlotte. It is a young woman brilliant with the jewels of a bride.

Is that lair of wild beasts of the desert, then, the palace in which the wedding of the daughter of an emir will be completed?

"Why are you remaining silent, my beloved?" murmurs the virgin of Yemen. "Since we have seen the domes of my natal city disappear, you have been as bleak and silent as an angel of tombs; you have not addressed a word to me to reassure my uncertain soul."

"How could I have words of consolation on my lips, when the thoughts of my heart prophesy mourning and death?"

"Is that my recompense, ingrate? If you're pursued by a regret, it's that of having snatched me from the death that I was about to give myself; the misfortune that your thought prophesy is the tedium of being burdened with a poor girl whose aspect importunes you."

"Leila, Leila, I love you more than the blessed, whom I shall never see, love their divine houris. I would have given my share of paradise for one of your kisses, when I had one for which to hope."

Leila had only listened to the first part of his statement. She tipped back her pretty head on the stranger's knees, and her little hands seized the falling creases of his hood.

"Don't hide your face thus, like an Imam when he comes to the tent to pray on Friday. Look at me with your mad eyes."

"Oh," stammered the terrified hadji, "child, do you want to take a scorpion in your soft hand, to play with a sharp damascene blade?"

But she had already uncovered the hadji's pale face, and her hands, crossed over the stranger's nape, drew his face toward hers.

The stranger's reason was troubled; he threw his arms around the young woman, and in their long ecstasy his gaze devoured her with all their flames. Their cheeks touched, their mouths united, quivering; then he lifted his wild gaze again in order to contemplate her anew. Leila sometimes felt sparks springing forth in her arteries and setting fire to her entire body, their sharp darts starring in all directions, sometimes a heavy cold gripping her heart like an icy hand; sometimes she was agitated, prey to an extraordinary delirium, sometimes she fell back, dying and annihilated.

✳

He got up abruptly, passing his hand over his brow like a man returning to his senses after an agitated dream. Leila was sitting on the palm leaves; her head fell back, exhausted, against the wall of the grotto; her lips were discolored, and the vivacity of her beautiful eyes, ringed by black circles, was seen to fade away gradually.

He uttered a cry, a cry so terrible and superhuman that wandering lions responded to it in the distance with fearful roars, and, falling full length, he rolled at Leila's feet, biting the earth and tearing it with his fingernails.

"I've killed her!" he roared. "I've killed her! The prediction is accomplished! It was written! Malediction upon the angel who has written it in the iron book! Malediction upon the prophet and his race! Malediction upon me!"

Leila raised her languid head.

"What's the matter with you, my husband?" she said to him. "You don't know what I'm experiencing; my heart is going away; but why do you say that it's you? Why are you blaspheming the holy name of the prophet?"

"Listen!" he cried. "I am the enchanter Il Haboul;[1] versed in the sciences that reveal to the physicist the most hidden secrets of creation and submit it to the occult forces of nature, I succeeded in giving my gaze the irresistible power of fascination. I used it to seduce the wife of a descendant of the prophet!"

A profound sigh interrupted him; Leila's head slumped on to her breast. "I seduced her," he cried, in a heart-rending voice, "but I didn't love her."

---

1 Il Haboul is a character in one of the continuations of Galland's *Mille-et-une nuits*, but the name had also been employed by the mystic proto-Romantic Jacques Cazotte.

Leila raised her eyes toward him again.

"The outraged Emir knew my crime; he could not kill me, but he cursed me. 'Go,' he said to me, 'your gaze, which fascinates hearts, will not lose its fatal power. You can still make yourself loved, but you will give death when you love. Go, take with you the evil eye!'

"I was returning from a pilgrimage to Mecca, undertaken in order to try to obtain mercy from the prophet, when I saw you for the first time. And I've killed you! I've killed you! You're going to expire before my eyes, and your last thought will be a thought of horror for me, for the monster that has withered your youth, who has devoured your life, like a hideous vampire!"

"Come here," said Leila, in a faint voice.

He dragged himself to her on his knees.

"Have you ever loved anyone but me?"

"No."

She put her enfeebled arms around his neck.

"I forgive you, friend. You can see that I'm not suffering; it's a very mild death. I don't regret dying thus. Isn't it better to die young than to go slowly with the years, to feel love ebbing away slowly from a heart chilled by age? I've loved you; I've been happy, I have no complaint now. I'm only sad because of you, for you'll be unhappy when I am no more."

He burst into sobs, bathing her with tears,

and clasping her to his bosom, with anguish, as if to dispute her with the angel of death.

She spoke to him thus for the rest of the night, more gently and more tenderly as she felt the flame of life dying within her by degrees; and when the dawn appeared she closed her eyes, collapsed in her lover's arms, and her soul departed with the first rays of sunlight.

He gazed at her for some time in silence; then, suddenly, uttering a discordant and insensate burst of laughter, he cried: "Ah! Ah! Imbecile emir, you forgot the best of your vengeance. You did not think of the means to prevent me from following her!"

And, drawing his dagger, he plunged it to the hilt into his heart.

A few days later, a desert Arab, having chanced to go into the cavern, discovered the bodies of the two lovers, still holding one another in an embrace. Transported by avaricious joy at the sight of the young woman's rich ornaments, he was about to bear a sacrilegious hand to her remains when a cry of terror escaped him. He had thought that he had seen the other cadaver gazing at him with fixed and flamboyant eyes. He withdrew, tottering, seized by a strange vertigo.

The evil eye had conserved its power, even in death.

THE WYVERN

Chapter I

HOLY and marvelous was Christmas Eve when the village church loomed up on the horizon between the confused clumps of ash trees and lindens, with its ogives and fiery rose-windows, while a thousand stars in the firmament and a thousand torches in the ancient nave illuminated the celebration of the good news marvelously in the heavens and on earth. Only the voices of those singing: "Come, let us rejoice in the Lord" to the naïve tune of ancient times, played by a panharmonic organ, and the bleating of the symbolic lamb troubled the silence of the mysterious hour, like the celestial choir that announced to the shepherds the birth of a God.

The festival was beautiful that year. A light frost had hardened the mud of the streets and the sky was a blue as a royal mantle, so no one had failed to respond to the joyous appeal of the bells and the entire parish was gathered, from the village patriarch to a child still drawn along on his grandmother's spinning-wheel.

The prior was flamboyant at the altar in his ceremonial cope. The altar, the vases and the silver-plated Christ seemed to be surrounded by a large aureole. The devotees had lit candles before their favorite saints in candle-holders whose arms were deployed like the seven-branched menorahs of the Hebrew prophet. The venerable faces of the elders seated in the choir-stalls were beaming under their long gray hair at the peaceful joys brought to them by the sacred canticles; even the boys and girls only looked at one another occasionally, laughing, and remained atten- tive and devotional for long intervals. In brief, never had so much pomp and meditation sanctified the old church.

Only one person present did not seem to be sharing the pious disposition of the audience, and his vague and wandering gaze revealed a soul attached to something other than the mystery whose commemoration was resounding around him. Pierre was not reputed among good souls, however, to be impious or libertine. He was a handsome enough fellow, laborious and agile, as robust and bold as one of the king's man-at-arms, who feared neither the *moine-bourreau*[1] or the werewolf, living in good repute and renown in the region, although a trifle covetous and entertaining loftier ideas and ambitions than befit a simple farmer, but as good a Christian thus far as you or I.

Tonight, though, he had strange distractions. Ordinarily, he placed himself being the cantor in order to follow on the euphonaire,[2] from beginning to end, the partition of the great festivals, but he his turned his eyes away, summoned in vain by the scarlet and azure characters and the gigantic notes of the plainsong, or, if he looked at something on the lectern I believe—God forgive me—that it was the old wooden eagle that sustained it on its outspread wings. He usually responded in a tone so full and sonorous to the falsetto voices of the children of the choir, knowing responses in prose and verse that could match

---

1 The *moine-bourreau* [hangman monk] is a bogeyman mentioned in several other Romantic works of the period, apparently derived from French translations of Benvenuto Cellini's memoirs, also cited therefrom by Goethe.

2 This word does not seem to exist anywhere but in the present text; it is presumably the "panharmonic organ" previously mentioned, but that reference is equally obscure.

any chaplain or cantor for twenty leagues around, but he now maintained a bleak silence—or, if habit sometimes caused him to open his mouth mechanically, he intoned the *Miserere* while the entire parish was repeating *Te deum laudamus*.

But then, if he was having thoughts regarding Marguerite that were not given by Heaven; if it were her for whom his anxious eyes were searching in the crowd, the good God would doubtless forgive him; she was so good and so pretty, and Pierre owed her so much gratitude. Had not the daughter of the rich Géraud preferred the amour of the poor farmer to that of his opulent rivals, even a proud bourgeois of the commune, an alderman of the neighboring village?

But no, the pale Marguerite was fully occupied with the divine office and the beribboned lamb that she was leading, in accordance with custom, to midnight mass and Pierre's gaze had not attempted to meet hers; it was plunging vaguely into places where the candles only cast a dubious light; it was wandering in the aisles of the nave and the somber wings of the Gothic edifice, following the great arches that spanned the vault, projecting bizarre *culs-de-lampe* at their junctions, and losing itself in the indecisive sculptures of the organ-case.

He seemed to be waiting for some fantastic apparition to glide between the columns or to suspend itself from the vault.

Oh, Pierre, Pierre! You are thinking too much about nocturnal tales!

Suddenly, his pupils dilated extraordinarily; his jaw dropped and his respiration stopped! A kind of flash had attracted his gaze toward an immense rose-window with innumerable compartments, and on the colored panes, brilliant with the interior light of the church, he thought he had seen the shadow of an elongated form snaking; he thought he had seen two wings agitating resplendently, like a red flame.

And when the priest had descended from the altar and the congregation was flowing noisily from the broad porch like water gushing from the mouth of a cavern at the ebb tide, Pierre came out with the crowd, but did not follow it. He backed up against the niche of a saint and remained there, immobile and pensive.

However, Marguerite's father had invited him to the nocturnal feast; sparkling cider and *gateaux à quatre pieds* were waiting for him beside his darling; and when she passed close to him as she quit the church she called to him softly in a sweet voice—but he did not hear her.

When he was alone, it seemed to him that the eccentric figures that the sculptor had caused to project horizontally between the buttresses were shaking their horned heads at him and staring at him with their stone eyes.

Finally, he withdrew, slowly, but it was too late to go and see Marguerite and eat *gateaux à quatre pieds*.

That is what comes of listening to an old shepherd sorcerer on the eve of the Nativity

On the eve of Saint-Ives, as the bells were ringing to announce the advent of Noël, Pierre had encountered old Anceaume on the edge of the wood.

Anceaume knew strange things. Where had he learned them? No one could say, for he was new to the region, but there was no doctor of astrology or alchemy who could have contended with him. And he loved Pierre, because Pierre listened gladly to his marvelous stories and had spent days and nights listening to tales of people who changed iron and copper into gold or who discovered hidden treasures with a hand of glory or a forked hazel-wand.

If Pierre had been a prudent and wise man he would have saluted the fellow politely—for it is always necessary to be polite to everyone, even sorcerers—and then gone tranquilly on his way, for such an encounter, at such an hour, near a thicket where holly and vervain flourished, had something suspect about it; but Pierre was not so sage; on the contrary, he went straight to the old man and asked him resolutely: "Well, old man, how are you?"

"Hum!" grunted Anceaume. "How am I? Fine, if I were twenty years old; I'd have the hope of making a fortune, becoming a castellan or a baron. But at present, old and decrepit as I am, what good would it do me? I'm no longer spry enough to attempt the enterprise. Oh, if I'd seen sixty years ago what I've seen this evening . . ."

"What have you seen, then, Père Anceaume?"

"I've seen the Wyvern," the shepherd replied.

"The Wyvern!" said Pierre.

And Père Anseaume told him that the Wyvern only appeared in the region once every hundred years, and that when it went to drink at the springs, at moonrise, it laid its magic carbuncle down on the grass, and that the man who was clever enough to take possession of that stone while the Wyvern was occupied in drinking would become the possessor of inexhaustible riches, and could not be put to death by iron, by fire, or the waves.

And he had seen it pass over the wood that evening.

Oh, Pierre, you think too much about nocturnal tales.

"Pierre, your fig-trees are frost-bitten, because you haven't wrapped them in straw during the night."

"Pierre, the weevils have eaten the wheat that you put in my grain-loft, because you haven't come to turn it over,"

"Pierre, you nourish your cow poorly, for her milk is becoming bitter and devoid of cream, and the ladies of the château no longer want it."

That was what the neighbors said to him in passing; then they went on, shaking their heads, always seeing him sitting at his table, his eyes in his fists.

One other person said nothing, but had a heavy heart because of Pierre's conduct. He scarcely showed himself for a quarter of an hour from time to time at Père Géraud's house, and scarcely addressed a few words of amity to poor Marguerite. She was not deceived by them; she could see only too well that while his mouth was speaking to her, his mind was far away.

That had dragged on for a fortnight. In the meantime, Pierre remained shut up at home all day long, and when dusk fell he went through the fields, no one knew where.

Often, when the moon rose over the horizon, dull and surrounded by a ruddy circle, the wind whistled and roared through the leafless skeletons of the oaks and beeches, whipping his face, and the wolves howled around him, he ran like a specter through the deserted countryside. Then he lay down in his woolen cloak in the depths of a deep ravine near some lively spring, and there he gazed by turns at the sky and the spring, until the moon had reached the culminating point of its course; then he got up, somber and dejected, and went home at a slow pace.

In fact, his bold enterprise had very little chance of success. More than one spring seethed in the vicinity; of which one was the Wyvern particularly fond? That was what he could not even discover. His brilliant hopes diminished every night, without the fury of his desires lowering with them. An ardent fever was devouring him.

Only one spring remained for him to visit; it was a trickle of water that idled between a few willows. Local tradition had consecrated it to an old saint whose statue dominated the reinforcement of bricks that the villagers had given to that natural trough of the neighboring flocks.

One evening, resolved to tempt fortune one last time, he went to establish himself behind the willows some distance from the spring of Saint Wilbert.

He heard nothing but the cries of the rooks that were croaking as they dreamed in the branches of the willows; he saw nothing in the air but the large white clouds that rolled one after another over the nocturnal crescent, covering it with a transparent shroud of gauze. His bleak and discouraged gaze wandered in space.

By dint of letting his eyes wander among the vague figures of the clouds, one little cloud ended up attracting his attention; its mobile and multiple forms stood out more clearly and were colored more vividly than any of its neighbors. Sometimes it rounded out in a sphere whose empty interior allowed a glimpse of the starry sky; sometimes it extended and elongated immeasurably; its thin extremity resembled the yellow tail of a snake; light wisps were deployed on its back like two wings, and its head, doubtless scintillating in the moon's rays, seemed to agitate a crown of flames.

That's a singular cloud, Pierre said to himself.

He saw it then detach itself from the nebulous army and advance like a whirlwind across the sky; and as it approached, its aspect become both more distinct and more extraordinary; its body was spangled with blue, green and yellow; it was surely on dentellate wings that it was sustaining itself in the air; for feet armed with sharp claws emerged from its shiny abdomen, and its head brightened the space around it with a ruddy radiance. And Pierre saw that the cloud was a huge winged serpent, which bore on its crest a carbuncle as resplendent as the sun.

His heart was beating as if it were about to break through his chest.

The Wyvern settled on the frozen snow, which crackled under the weight of the marvelous beast, and reddened in the distance as if with the reflection of a great fire. The Wyvern furled its long sulfurous wings, crouched down, and, taking its carbuncle between its two forepaws, placed it in a furrow three paces away from the last willow; then it ran to the spring.

The fatal moment had arrived; it was necessary to perish or to take possession of the talisman. Pierre felt almost faint, but one glance at the dazzling stone, which cast more light over the vicinity than a hundred torches, rendered him courage. Fortunately, he was behind the penultimate willow; he crept silently toward the furrow in which the carbuncle lay; then, three paces away, when nothing any longer hid him from the Wyvern's eyes, he suddenly stood up in order to launch himself with a single bound upon the object of so many desires and late nights.

The Wyvern had perceived him!

At the same instant, it turned round with the rapidity of a tempest; a horrible, immense whistle rattled in its hoarse throat; its lips were drawn back, uncovering all its sharp white teeth all the way to the root; and, the jaws opening to their full width, it leapt toward the reckless man . . .

Chapter II

Marguerite was going sadly along the great avenue of the château.

Her fresh cheeks had paled, her brilliant eyes were reddened and dulled by tears, for misfortune had weighed upon her family for a year. Scab-rot had killed her father's sheep, the fire of heaven had devoured his farm; his cows and horses had died in the conflagration, and a hurricane had flattered and destroyed his wheat.

The rich Géraud had not been able to pay the new lord either the annual rent or the rightful welcome; threatened with being expelled from his ancestral roof and sick with chagrin and despair, he had said to his daughter: "Go, my child, and find the noble baron who has just acquired the fief of our former seigneur. Perhaps he will accord to your tears the delay that my white hair could not obtain from his steward."

The poor girl's heart bled at the thought of the poverty that threatened her aged father after so many years of labor. Alas, she had no need of those further troubles.

She went over the drawbridge and remained for a long time in the interior courtyard of the château, hesitant and not daring to go into the apartments until an old majordomo, taking pity on her embarrassment, asked her the reason for her coming, and, leading her through splendid rooms filled with pages and richly-equipped gentlemen, introduced her to the seigneur's presence.

Marguerite stopped, dazzled and tottering; all the colors of the rainbow trembled in confused circles in her eyes, as if she were looking directly at the sun.

What she saw would have struck the admiration of a queen; with what astonishment the simple girl could not help being seized!

Golden arabesques framed a ceiling painted entirely with the precious azure of ultramarine and dotted with silver stars. The wall-panels were covered with tapestries of a miraculous magnificence and workmanship, but the personages depicted there were as bizarre and fantastic as the phantoms of our dreams, and no subject from the Holy Scriptures could be seen there.

Near a sandalwood table, covered in golden and crystal vases, in an armchair whose delicate sculptures were encrusted with precious stones, the noble suzerain reposed, enveloped in a long robe of blue-green velvet, trimmed with ermine and embroidered with rubies.

Marguerite's guide approached the noble baron and begged him to grant an audience to the supplicant. A haughty and distracted nod of the head responded to his request.

Marguerite knelt down on the mosaic floor tiles.

"Alas, alas, my good seigneur, take pity on an old man from whom the bread of his last days has been stolen. Take pity on a poor girl whose heart is broken by chagrin since she has lost her lover, Pierre. The demon has taken him from me, body and soul; God grant that he be delivered! A perfidious magician has taken him away to the land of the damned. Since that hour of desolation, the hand of the Accursed One had not withdrawn from above us."

Encouraged by the attention that appeared to be lent to her, she became sufficiently emboldened to raise her eyes to the baron and his majordomo. A piercing cry escaped her breast.

"God forgive me! It's my lover Pierre who is listening to me under those royal vestments! It's the aged Anceaume who is looking at me with his sorcerer's smile!"

The baron's face had darkened momentarily, but a flash of pleasure chased the shadows from his brow and a fire rose to his cheeks. He looked at his majordomo. The latter's eyebrows were raised, the corner of his mouth rose singularly, and he laughed. Then he drew away.

"Yes, I'm your lover Pierre, Marguerite, my sweet darling. I'm that Pierre, who loves you as Pierre the shepherd loved you."

He had drawn the young woman into his arms, who contemplated him, motionless and open-mouthed, as if she had seen a spirit appear.

"Pierre! Pierre!" she exclaimed, struggling against his kisses, "is it really you? Have you not sold your soul for all this glory?"

"No," he said. "All this is legitimately acquired; but let's leave that for now; let's only think of the happiness of belonging to one another!"

"Let me go, Pierre! Can you, a rich and powerful castellan, still be the husband of poor Géraud's daughter?"

"Yes, you are my wife, my beloved wife!"

The weary head of the village girl fell upon the baron's shoulder . . .

✳

"Well, what have you done with the demoiselle?" asked the steward Anceaume.

"I've sent her home to console her father. She'll keep the secret. She'll come back tomorrow."

"May one know monseigneur's intentions in her regard?"

"My intentions, damn it! Do you know, Anceaume, that Marguerite is a sweet and genteel flower? She's never delighted me as much as she does today. In fact, why shouldn't I keep my word to her? I have treasures and honors enough to live happily and grandly. The girl would have shared with me before; what if I were to share with her now?"

"That would be the action of a grateful and Christian soul," replied Anceaume, with an expression of compunction to make one shiver. "I hope not to be the last to congratulate the beautiful bride and Master Géraud the farmer."

Pierre frowned.

"It is monseigneur's prerogative," Anceaume continued, "to give new examples to the neighboring barons. They have narrow and petty minds. They'll protest and complain about that misalliance, but isn't it one pleasure more to excite the reprobation of the vulgar? The scorn of fools is, they say, the treasure of the sage."

The castellan stirred in his seat. Each of those words pricked his proud heart like a sharp needle.

"Comtesse Blanche is very beautiful," Anceaume went on. "Her skin is more dazzling than ermine, her cheeks fresher than an eglantine rose. Comtesse Blanche is the suzeraine of ten castellanies, held in faith and homage by ten banner-carrying knights; fleur-de-lys shine in her blazon, because she is a cousin on the distaff side of his highness King Charles of France."

"Well," murmured Messire Pierre, "so what?"

"Twenty seigneurs of the foremost houses in the realm dispute the title of servant to the noble lady, but there is one knight whose pursuit would have more chances than all the rest put together; however, that knight, little desirous of what the crowd wants, prefers the bonnet of a village girl to the golden hennin of the comtesse, for he has an independent soul that is above the prejudices of society."

"Satan!" cried the baron.

"Ahem," said Anceaume. "That knight is Messire Pierre de Saint-Wilbert, the beloved of Comtesse Blanche, the lover of the peasant-girl Marguerite."

"What does all this signify?" stammered the castellan, agitatedly. "Me, the preferred of the comtesse? Where is the proof?"

"The proof? My colleague Hirboud, the geomancer, the savant Bohemian, will give it to you when you wish. She has been to consult him in your regard; she has begged him to discover, by the power of his art, whether you would be loyal and faithful in amour. He has not failed to inform me of it, and he has responded in consequence."

Messire Pierre stood up, as if he would have liked to strike the ceiling on the room with his head. His eyes were sparkling; his breast swelled with a superb joy; and, squeezing forcefully a little lemon-wood casket that he wore around his neck suspended on a chain of diamonds, he cried: "O my carbuncle, I shall be the cousin of the king!"

Marguerite came back the next morning; she had become rosy again, crimson and brilliant; her eyes had recovered their gentle flame, her lips their infantile smile. As light as a bird, she traversed the apartments filled with gentlemen and pages, no longer dazzled by anything, and not asking her way.

"Pierre, my Pierre, it's me, your Marguerite! Can't you see me? Are you dreaming again, as of old?"

The castellan was as grave and somber as the figures on his tapestries.

"Pierre, when will you go to see old Abbé Godefroy, who loved you so much when you sang in the choir? What pleasure he will have in seeing you again, fortunate and powerful! It's from him, isn't it, that you will order our marriage mass? When will the candles burn on the altar with our intention?"

"I shall not go to request prayers from Abbé Godefroy, and candles will not be lit on the altar for our marriage mass, for I am not your lover Pierre."

Marguerite opened her eyes very wide, and did not understand.

"I am not a shepherd; I am the Sire de Saint-Wilbert, chevalier, and future spouse of Comtesse Blanche."

Marguerite's face became as pale and wan as that of a corpse.

The baron's voice took on, involuntarily, a softer tone, almost tender.

"However, girl, I have profited from your error, and I shall not abandon you if you wish to remain close to me: I shall add you to the number of the comtesse's servants, and I shall sometimes see you in private . . . unknown to the noble lady."

Marguerite made no response; she trembled twice, and then launched herself with the rapidity of a bolt chased by the cord of an arbalest.

"As you wish," murmured the baron, in an ill-humored tone.

A week later, a splendid cavalcade traversed the village. Messire Pierre went forth in great pomp toward the domains of his illustrious fiancée. As he went past the church, his cortege crossed the path of another, less pompous and less rapid, which was emerging from the abode of God to go to that if the dead. The procession was following two coffins, one white and one black.

The disappearance and supposed death of her lover had already undermined the frail organism of Marguerite; his treason had killed her.

Her father had only survived her by twenty-four hours.

✳

Messire Pierre is the husband of the comtesse, and one of the great barons of the kingdom.

Messire Pierre has gold enough to pave his entire château, including the courtyard and stables, and seigneuries that one cannot traverse without changing horizon ten times.

He is on the best of terms with the uncles of King Charles; Monsieur de Berry smiles at him graciously and Monsieur de Bourgogne calls him his good cousin.[1]

In brief, his prosperity has become proverbial, and it is said throughout France, as a popular manner of speaking: "As lucky as the Sire de Saint-Wilbert."

However, the baron is singularly taciturn, and never laughs, doubtless because good fortune is the enemy of noisy gaiety.

If quarrels are the wind that revives the flame of amour, the mutual passion of the castellan and his beautiful wife must sigh very rarely.

---

1 This reference implies that the King Charles to whom reference is made is Charles VI (1368-1422), who came to the throne as a child in 1380, after which France was ruled by a regency including Philippe, Duc de Bourgogne, Jean, Duc de Berry and Louis I, Duc d'Anjou.

Neither fêtes, nor tourneys, pleasures and new fortunes, could extract Messire Pierre from his morose humor. His only joy was leaning his elbow on his table and considering his carbuncle for hours on end.

He believed that he perceived that he was not alone in taking pleasure in that contemplation; he believed that he divined that Anceaume was seeking, under various pretexts, to introduce himself into his presence at those moments. He surprised gazes whose strange gleam had not been dulled by age, and which seemed, when they fell upon it, to embrace the carbuncle with a more ardent redness.

Anceaume was sent as majordomo to a distant castellany, which the baron had just acquired.

Some time after that, one night when Messire Pierre had been awake and pensive for a long time—God knows why—and he became drowsy in his armchair, a slight sound, alike that of a person sliding stealthily along the paneling, extracted him from his somnolence. He listened, motionless, piercing the shadows with the eagle gaze that he darted through eyelids that were not quite closed.

By the confused gleam of his night-lamp he glimpsed a figure advancing toward him with precaution, and a ray of light fell upon the thin and wrinkled face of old Anceaume. At the moment when he arrived oblique; at the baron's seat, the latter stood up abruptly. With one hand he lifted the majordomo over the arm of the chair and laid him down at his feet; with the other he drew his dagger.

"Mercy," murmured the old man, choking under two iron knees that were crushing his chest. "Mer . . . cy!" The last syllable of the word, commenced via the ordinary conduit of the voice, emerged in a hiss through a new passage that had just been opened. The cold steel had cut Anceaume's throat.

"Take that, carbuncle thief!" said the castellan.

Anceaume was dead, and yet his two eyes were staring at his murderer, fixed, haggard and wide open.

Pierre closed them with his bloody hand, but he had scarcely done so than the right eye opened again and directed at the baron a frightful wink of irony and malevolence.

"Curse you!" said the castellan, as he closed the rebellious eye again. The left had opened again, more atrocious than its neighbor!

"Dog of a sorcerer, even after your death!" cried Pierre. He went to fetch from his arsenal the counterweight of a trebuchet, opened the window, attached the wooden block to the neck of the cadaver, and threw both of them into the deep moat of the château.

The head of the shepherd reappeared among the reeds, with his eyes of fire and his sniggering mouth, and then sank.

Messire Pierre did not sleep that night.

Chapter III

It was a singular household, that of the Sire de Saint-Wilbert and Comtesse Blanche.

Since the early times of their union, those two haughty and irascible spirits had suffered daily collision and friction. There are sometimes, in past life, memories that cause blushes to redden the face and embitter the heart. An unfortunate hazard, doubtless, incessantly put those fatal allusions into the lady's mouth.

No one knew better how to launch sharp sarcasm, in a milder and more gracious voice, at the heart that she wanted to wound; no one turned her pretty iron fingers more nonchalantly in the wounds that she had inflicted.

Pierre, incessantly the butt of her poignant gaiety, resembled a bull roaring with rage under the prod of the child guiding it.

Finally, one day when she had tormented him excessively, he cried: "My God, Madame, it's time that all this finished; I'm weary of serving as your quintain, and besides, it's not by remaining chained to a woman's apron that a true knight achieves renown. Monsieur Loys de Bourbon[1] is preparing to battle against the miscreants of Thunes; I shall accompany him, and we'll see when I return whether absence has blunted the darts of your tongue."

"Go, Messire; perhaps, in that distant region, you'll rediscover your noble family!"

Pierre ran out of the apartment; he was choking. The following week, he and his contingent had joined the host of the Duc de Bourbonnais.

The sun is descending, red and devoid of radiance behind the blue chains of the Atlas.

Errant vapors are carrying through the atmosphere the odors of carnage and death's crimson-tinted streams are snaking like long

---

1 Louis II, Duc de Bourbon, another of Charles VI's uncles, who launched the "Barbary crusade" against Tunisian pirates in 1390 during a lull in the Hundred Years War; like Charles VI, he was reputed to be mad. Froissart's chronicle includes an account of the crusade in question.

veins over the yellow sand, and precipitating, seething, into limpid springs, which they change into bloody swimming-baths. Among the hillocks charged with date-palms other, artificial and semi-living dunes rise here and there; it is the frantic hands of men that have just formed those mounds with human cadavers.

The battle is now over; they have been fighting all day, helm against turban, sword against scimitar, the heavy lance against the light spear. The day has been terrible, for three Moorish kings were there with all the forces of their kingdoms and the warriors of Islam attacked as numerously as the waves of the sea; but the victory has remained with Christ and Duc Loys, and the emirs of the green banners, the red pirates of Tunis and Djair, the Berbers of the mountains and the savage Kabyles lie in thousands on the plain, where triumphant fanfares resonate in all parts, recalling the Northern cavaliers to their pennants.

One of the barons does not respond to the signal of the Christian trumpets What has become of the Sire de Saint-Wilbert? He was seen throughout the battle plunging into the thick of the melee, cleaving iron skull-caps and thrusting through coats of mail with his fine sword. His breastplate and his shield were bristling with darts, like the back of a porcupine, and his weapons chipped in a thousand places by axes and yataghans, but not a drop of blood soiled his armor except that of Muslims.

Messire Pierre, at the end of the action, had persisted in the pursuit of a few Tripolitan horsemen who were fleeing the battlefield. On their heels he traversed valleys and hills; he followed them for a long time but the African chargers finally wearied his Norman destrier; the exhausted animal became rebellious to the spur, and the knight was obliged to stop in a great plain of sand, which he had just entered on emerging from a defile between two crags.

He reposed for a while with his horse and then tried to rediscover his route and return to the army, but it was in vain. Hills, ravines and valleys intersected and entwined around him all night long, and when dawn came he found himself in the desert of sand again.

Then he was hungry and thirsty, for he had not taken any nourishment since the morning before the battle, and his throat was desiccated by fatigue and dust.

He scanned the plain with a circular gaze as far as his sight could reach; no verdant bush interrupted the monotonous pallor of the solitude to indicate the well of nomadic flocks.

Only spiny shrubs appeared at intervals, gray and dusty, but no crown of any broad-leaved fig-tree or the fans of a palm tree with red fruits.

Breathless and exhausted, Messire Pierre lay down on the fiery ground, under the iron sun. His armor burned him as if it had been heated red in a forge.

He took out his carbuncle from inside his surcoat and gazed at it silently. He must have had strange thoughts.

Merely by placing that prodigious stone on the ground he could cause gold coins to sprout therefrom, as if that new magnet attracted all the treasures of the king of the gnomes. By carrying it on his breast he had defied the wrath of men and that of the elements.

Now, it could not give him a drop of brackish water to prevent him from dying.

In that terrible moment, his past returned to his memory. He thought he could sense the coolness of the vaults of the parish church; he recalled the pretty stream on the banks of which he had once collected orchids and campanulas to decorate Marguerite's hair. He remembered the procession that had preceded his engagement.

Suddenly, raising his eyes, he perceived a man a few paces away whose back was turned to him, who seemed to be walking with difficulty because of his great age. He resembled an old marabout of the mountains.

Pierre did not even reflect on the singularity of that sudden apparition on flat and open ground. He raised himself up, with all the strength that remanded to him, and launched himself toward the old man.

"Infidel," he cried, hoarsely. "Give me that bread and the gourd that you have under your arm."

"Oho, Messire, does your carbuncle not give anything to eat and drink to those who are hungry and thirsty?"

And the marabout, turning round, let the stupefied baron see the hideous wrinkled face of Anceaume.

"Heaven and Hell!" cried the knight. "Are we, then, on the day of the resurrection of the dead?"

"Not that I know, my good seigneur," the ex-majordomo replied, "but the Eternal Father has consented to make a small individual miracle in my favor; or, if you prefer, you noble hand only partially severed the throat of your humble servant—as you wish."

"Man or devil, dead or alive, give me your bread and your gourd."

"Not so fast, if you please, Monseigneur. I have become a trader in my old age, you see, and I don't deliver anything for nothing. What will you give me for my bread and my gourd?"

"What do you want? Speak, quickly."

"Your carbuncle, Messire. It's purely for economy; it will spare me oil and tallow during my late nights."

"Wretch!"

The baron tried to throw himself upon the old shepherd, but the latter slid between his hands with a briskness astonishing for his age. He stopped some distance away and, lifting the objects of Pierre's desire toward him, grimacing and sniggering, he repeated: "Your carbuncle, Messire!"

Pierre leapt at him again, but he escaped again. Twenty times he was on the point of seizing him, but twenty times, as he put his hand on his collar, he suddenly saw him ten paces ahead, behind, to the left or the right.

He let himself fall to the ground again, incapable of making another movement. Anceaume approached very close to him and suspended the bread and the gourd over his head.

"Listen," stammered Pierre. "Would you

like lands, châteaux, seigneuries? Would you like tonnes of gold? You shall have them."

"No; your carbuncle."

"Take it, then," murmured the knight, with a dull groan; and he held out the precious stone.

Anceaume seized it, and threw him the price.

Then Anceaume's thin nose elongated into a muzzle with ardent nostrils; his mouth with turned-up corners split into a fanged maw; his feet and hands became paws armed with claws; his garments changed into colored scales, and two large clawed wings unfurled on his shoulders.

The carbuncle blazed on his forehead like a meteor.

"Do you recognize me, Pierre?" howled the monster. "I am the Wyvern; I am the eldest daughter of the father of all serpents. I let you take my carbuncle for nothing; you have returned it to me for bread and water. I am more generous than you. Now drink and eat if you wish! My water is bitter and my bread full of ash. Ullah!"

Pierre uttered a frightful howl and expired, blaspheming the holy name of God.

"Mine, body and soul!" roared the Wyvern. It placed its paw on the body of the unfortunate man, and struck the ground with its wing.

The earth opened up, and howls of joy were heard in the abysms. Satan's daughter was swallowed up with her prey in the fiery dungeons at the center of the globe.

ISUREN
A Story taken from the Annals of Kachmyr

Fulmen detulit in terras mortalibus ignem
Primitus; inde omnis flammarum
deditus ardor.
—Lucretius. *De rerum natura.*

IT was in the ancient ages that followed the retreat of the waters of the deluge. The old Ocean, on reentering the vast bed from which it had emerged more than once to conquer the rest of the world, had left behind it on the drying surface of the continents deep layers of alluvial mud in which the seeds of a powerful and disorderly life were fermenting, and the face of the globe had soon disappeared almost entirely under the rapid eruption of a prodigious vegetation. The earth was no longer anything but a limitless forest, impenetrable to daylight, where humans appeared at intervals, wandering like exiles over the new soil that covered the empires and cities of their forefathers.

The antediluvian generations had taken away the sciences and arts of the world that no longer existed; the pale reflection of traditions had been effaced by degrees and then extinguished in a profound night; social bonds were forgotten, even those of the family dissolved, and the unfortunate survivors of the human race wandered, weak, scarce, naked and isolated, ignorant of the sun and God. They slipped through thickets like wild beasts, under the black shade that spread an eternal twilight over them, or crawled through marshes and jungles like filthy reptiles emerging from the waters of the deluge, alternately devouring the bloody flesh of animals weaker than themselves, when they lacked acorns and berries—the use of fire having long been unknown to them—or devoured by the stronger, for they were unaware of the glorious inventions that give humans hard metal and the blind forces of nature for defenders.

The rays of the setting sun, fragmented by the crowns of gigantic trees by which immense mountains were veiled, then nameless among humans, enabled a dull half-light to penetrate between the branches and interlaced lianas, which scarcely reached the ground bristling with rude and vivacious plants.

Strange noises rose and fell, prolonged over the steep slopes of highlands; marvelous spectacles succeeded one another in their abysms of verdure; the harmonious coïl[1] sang between the branches of mangroves; great white oxen with superb horns, black and hideous bison and impetuous unicorns passed, bellowing and whinnying, through the tamarisks, coconut palms and alleimarams; beautiful swans rose up like white clouds from the midst of pink lotuses, to the rattle of nearby bamboos crushed under the heavy feet of the elephants that came to drink from the mountain springs.

Two human creatures, of different sexes, were lying in the long grass under the natural porticoes of an alleimaram[2] whose fecund branches covered the whole of a vast plateau. Both young, and beautiful in their savage nudity, the wise instinct that never intrudes into the monstrous aberrations of social con-

---

1 Author's note: "The black cuckoo of India."

2 Authors note: "The alleimaram, or banyan tree, throws out long branches parallel to the ground; at the extremity of each one, a bouquet of filaments forms, which then extend perpendicularly toward the ground, take root there and give birth to new trees still attached to the first."

ventions, had arranged their first amours well. Under the bushy black hair whose disorderly locks hid the young man's forehead, two ardent and staring eyes glinted; his gaze did not have the haggard astonishment of an animal's; the vague anxieties that they expressed took their source from intellectual depths unknown to the soul and contained them. Were they the almost effaced memory of a distant past or the presentiment of another existence, or perhaps both? One might have thought that his powerful torso was respiring poorly beneath those thick vaults, that the radiance of his eyes was breaking with indignation against the twenty-pace horizon.

But at the present moment the transports of pleasure and tenderness had replaced that habitual expression; almost inarticulate murmurs with caressant inflexions were emerging incessantly from his mouth, which had scarcely retained a few rare and simple words of the primitive language lost in the maze of Babel. Those two unfortunate beings had rediscovered Eden momentarily in the depths of their sad solitude.

The tyranny of needs did not take long to recall them to their precarious and difficult existence. The young woman lifted her head, supported on her companion's bosom, and addressed a few plaints to him, accompanied by a suppliant gaze.

Absorbed in his placid felicity, he did not seem to understand at first, but the word *hungry*, stammered insistently, finally reached his intelligence. He raised his eyes, but did not see any fruit hanging from the branches inclined over their couch or any cucurbitaceae creeping at their feet between the ferns.

He embraced his companion gently, and then bounded to his feet, trying to pierce with his gaze the curtains of foliage that surrounded him in all directions. He stamped his foot impatiently; then a memory seemed to clear the clouds from his brow and he departed like a wild stallion, breaking young cinnamon trees before him, tearing up the serpentine stems of pepper-trees enlaced with the multitudinous columns of the alleimaram.

He headed toward an area where the thicket, slightly cleared, had permitted a few banana trees to deploy their crowns of giant leaves freely. A cry of pleasure escaped him on rediscovering those precious trees almost respected by birds and monkeys; in all haste he took possession of a heavy cluster of bananas and resumed his course in the direction in which he had left his companion.

Suddenly, a short distance away, a hoarse cry became audible, a sort of dull growl, followed by a frightful mewling.

His hair stood on end, his pupils dilated with fear and he braced himself to flee . . .

He ended up darting like a snake in his original direction.

Night had fallen, as black as chaos, but he did not go astray.

Now a prolonged rustle ran through the thickets, and something—an oblong, bounding form—passed like lightning close to the young man. He thought he glimpsed a large animal carrying an indistinct object on its back.

He remained immobile, his tongue paralyzed, all his limbs dripping cold sweat, and then, uttering a cry more terrible than that of the ferocious beast, he tried to launch himself in its pursuit; but everything suddenly vanished, the noise and the running creature, and nothing responded to him but the wind in the mobile domes of the forest.

The unfortunate man rolled on the ground, uttering groans as lugubrious as those of a she-bear whose cubs have just been devoured by a hungry tiger.

Suddenly, during an interval that the exhaustion of his strength imposed on his plaints, it seemed to him that a weak and dolorous voice became audible nearby, like the echo of his own, so to speak.

He raised himself up on his hands, his neck extended and his ears alert, and almost immediately bounded toward that well-known voice.

At the same moment the forest resounded with the noise of a dull fall, followed by a splash of water; then there was the sound of a living being struggling against turbulent water.

The young man soon reappeared on the surface of the water, hanging on with one hand to the rough stems of fluvial plants, drawing after him with the other a seemingly-inanimate human body. It was that of his companion.

He set her down on the grass, streaming and chilled. His caresses recalled her to life, not without difficulty, and he understood from her words, punctuated with gestures of fear, that, seized by terror at the howls and the approach of the beast, her precipitate flight had caused her to fall into another danger, from which only the dense and sturdy plants garnishing the spring and her lover's help had extracted her.

Alas, if she had escaped the peril itself, she could not avoid its deadly consequences. The abrupt passage from violent fear to cold had disturbed her entire being; an icy frisson ran through her veins and her senses abandoned her again in the arms of her spouse.

The unfortunate man thought that she was dead; he applied his mouth to his companion's heart, and could no longer feel its beating under his lips.

His courage and strength were exhausted; he lay down next to her in order to die too.

It seemed to him that there would not be long to wait, for he sensed a lack of air in his lungs, and his respiration was struggling painfully against an oppression which he took to be that of death. The atmosphere was heavy and sulfurous, and long murmurs tan over the quivering plants and the lower branches of the trees, whose crowns fell silent.

Suddenly, an immense gust of wind launched forth, whistling, from the mountain summits, causing the innumerable population of vegetables that crowned all the slopes to bend over like a single stem. A dazzling light illuminated the most secret darkness of the woods; a prodigious, continuous, infinite detonation made even the rocks borne by the impenetrable terrestrial crust tremble.

The young man thought that the world was about to end with him and his beloved. He raised his head again; the air, less heavy, no longer drove his respiration back into his panting throat; the shadows had taken possession of the horizon almost entirely; a vivid radiation only arrived as far as him through the foliage of the alleimarans from the direction of a sheer peak covered with tuyas and somber yews.

He stood up, struck with amazement; a mechanical impulsion or some vague hope drew him toward that flamboyant light. He crossed the plateau rapidly and climbed the mountain on which the phenomenon was shining.

A large yew struck by lightning was agitating a plume of flame on the highest summit.

The savage recoiled fearfully; the fire from the sky, the only one that humans knew at the time, was only an object of horror for them: a supernatural being, malevolent and terrible, a divinity that they fled and did not worship.

But that movement of dread vanished in a flash; the mysterious essence could only give death!

The young man advanced slowly, frowning, and put out his arms with murmurs of anger toward the ardent tongues that were writhing and snaking around the tree.

As he drew closer, an extraordinary sensation penetrated his entire body; a mild warmth vivified his fatigued limbs, dried his hair soaked with water and sweat and insinuated itself into all his veins.

He continued walking, but that mild impression changed rapidly into a bitter, sharp and painful sensation. He recoiled again, and sat down on a stone silently, his head in his hands. An unusual travail was operating in his thought; his intelligence was seething within the narrow cortex that compressed it, striving to burst it into smithereens.

He shuddered sharply, went down the mountain and traversed the plateau again as if borne by the wings of an eagle. He found his inanimate companion, loaded her on to his shoulders and carried her, without being curbed by his burden for an instant, all the way to the summit that he had just quit.

Then, kneeling a few paces away from the blazing tree, he submitted her to the benevolent action whose salutary effects he had experienced himself, and waited, his lips parted, his heart palpitating and his anguished eyes fixed upon her.

Is it not a sweet and cruel illusion? A sigh—at least, it seems so—is exhaled feebly by the young woman's breast. A slight movement lifts up the immobile globes!

No, he is not mistaken, his companion's arms twitch; she moans, her eyelids open. She is alive! She is alive!

It was then that a God was revealed for the first time in the heart of the savage; in a spontaneous movement, irresistible and anterior to any reflection, he prostrated himself and worshiped that new power, which had announced itself by life and happiness!

While the two lovers abandoned themselves to the ineffable joys of such a reunion, distant thunder was still tumbling in the highlands; the clouds thickened and split, and the atmosphere, weary of their weight, precipitated them toward the earth in torrents of rain.

The inundation was as brief as it was impetuous. When the young savages emerged from a thicket where they had taken refuge, they saw their natural brazier almost extinct; black and opaque smoke had replaced its bright flames, and only a few branches were barely still alight, thanks to the protection of the dense branches of a neighboring tree.

An inspiration suddenly illuminated the young man's brain. He seized the inferior branches of the second tree and lowered them forcefully toward the diminished fire. The flame wrapped around that new aliment, spitting . . .

In an instant, a thousand jets darted from all parts around the bushy arms of the yew and rose along its resinous trunk. Soon, the entire tree was ablaze, a colossal candelabrum, the devouring splendor of which rapidly set fire to all its neighbors. Soon, the entire peak was nothing but a vast pyre covered by a dome of red smoke, from which a thousand ardent sparks sprang and spread out in all directions.

Having retreated to a nearby plateau with his companion, the young savage contemplated his work, his heart swollen by a sublime exaltation; but they were not alone, human beings ran from all parts of the forest, stupefied by admiration before such a spectacle.

In his curt and simple language, the young man recounted the benefits of fire to them.

"That which renders life ought no longer to die!" he cried. "Since it eats trees, let us always, always, give it trees for food. Humans, say with me: *Live forever, fire, friend of humans!*"

A universal acclamation greeted that harangue, the first that a human being had addressed to assembled humans, and all the human creatures introduced to that glorious mystery took one another by the hand and circled the burning mountain with an immense round-dance in honor of fire, the father of life, and Isuren, the inventor of fire.[1]

Suddenly, another voice replied to their joyous voices; through their songs of delight burst, like a horrible dissonance, a ferocious and staccato howling, and a monstrous tiger, bounding through the brushwood, came to fall, its maw open and its eyes bloody, fifty paces from Isuren.

Cries of alarm rose up everywhere; the hands parted; terror had broken the links of that living chain, interlaced for the first time. Everyone fled, forgetful of their fellows, while the monster, uncertain, paraded its gaze over so much prey offered to its rage.

"Stop!" cried Isuren. "If we flee, the beast is stronger than each of us. Let's attack it; all together, we're stronger than it is." And, seizing one of the flaming brands that the wind had chased to his feet, he fell upon the cruel animal, challenging its howls with a war cry.

Ten of the boldest among those who were fleeing returned in response to his appeal,

---

1 Author's note: "Among the Hindus, Isuren is fire personified; the root *ur*, conflagration, is found in all ancient languages."

and, in his example, precipitated themselves upon the tiger, which recoiled, growling before Isuren's blazing weapon. At the sight of new assailants, the ferocious beast made a sideways leap, charged one of them, knocked him down and, seizing him with it murderous claws, set about lacerating him; but Isuren had leapt forward, as light and terrible as the beast, and his ardent club descended like a tempest on the tiger's broad forehead.

The animal let go, spun round, and lay down on its side, panting, its red tongue hanging out; then it gathered its muscular legs, and launched itself, with a prodigious effort, ten paces from its adversaries, and fled, to the thunderous clamors of the victors; but an enormous stone, thrown by Isuren, struck it in mid-flight.

It rolled on the grass, dying, its spine broken.

Then the song of the first victory rose up, resonantly, toward the sky.

"Praise to Isuren, inventor of fire, vanquisher of the bloodthirsty tiger!"

"Listen to me," replied the new hero; "I am not the vanquisher of the tiger, but all of us have vanquished it. To maintain the fire, benefactor of humans, to vanquish our numerous enemies again, children of the same race, let us no longer separate; let us live united, on the same food and in the same retreats, and let us fight faithfully henceforth, the strong for the weak and the weak for the strong!"

"Let it be as you have said, Isuren, father of fire! You shall lead us from this day forth, and always, into combat against the beasts of the woods, and we will follow you, Isuren the strong and the sage!"

Thus, in that night of glory, the first society was born and the first state founded.

A north wind rose in the middle of the night, chasing southwards the rumbling tempests of the conflagration; it blew throughout the remainder of the darkness, if those resplendent hours could be called darkness.

The flames went forth, rolling their turbulent sheets and their great voice, like that of the waters of the deluge—a second deluge, in effect, which was to return to humans what the other had stolen. They went forth, and the expanses of forest, the bushy gorges and the stagnant marshes disappeared, swallowed up one after another by the waves of the ardent sea.

A thousand horrible and sublime sounds were confounded, like a single voice, in the roar of that red ocean. There was an endless crackling that was exhaled, like a death-rattle, by the entire vegetable population, and desiccated lakes dried up. There were the cries of despair of wild elephants, the mortal howls of tigers, the atrocious hissing of boas that writhed in their turn in the endless coils of serpents of fire, while the human race exulted, victoriously, on the mountain abandoned by the flames.

A less formidable brightness finally came to struggle in the sky against the vast reflection of the fire; the pale light of dawn inundated the firmament.

It was a glorious spectacle when the disk of the king of light rose slowly above the eastern mountains, when the sons of man saluted for the first time in many generations the dazzling star whose splendor the black vault of the woods no longer veiled.

Those beings, for whom the narrow interval between two impenetrable thickets had previously been the whole horizon, paraded their gaze, with amazement, over the infinite extent of the firmament and the vast regions of the earth. From the colossal peak where they seemed to be suspended from the sky, they saw extending beneath them immeasurable mountain chains covered in forests, which plunged from the highest summits into the depths of abysms; valleys of an incredible depth, into which impetuous rivers precipitated from the mountainsides; and then, toward the south, the sea of fire flowed incessantly, enlarging its bed with immense waves.

Then the genius, the precious seed of which the Eternal had deposited in the bosom of Isuren, was revealed entirely to the inventor of fire. He understood the world and himself, and the God that his heart had sensed was unveiled in his intelligence. It was in the name of the Universal Being, creator of the world open to their gaze, that he spoke to the new people, whose pontiff and legislator that it was about to be. Humans listened to his voice and worshiped with him the supreme essence, of which fire was the minister, and which had posed on its radiant throne in space in order to illuminate the earth and the air.

Following the conflagration like a guide, they descended after it from the height of the mountains. The sea of fire continued its route, launching toward all the winds of the sky the devouring rivers that were traveling the world; but the primitive conflagration, their father, rolled without deviation until it found a great sea before it. The two oceans battled; the humid plains swelled and boiled as if they were about to catch fire in their turn, but their ardent enemy was buried under their irritated waves.

Isuren's companions had stopped with him in a beautiful and rich valley irrigated by fecund streams. It was there, with the aid of the supreme wisdom, that he taught them the art of cultivating the precious gift of the earth, that of conserving, in the hollowed-out stems of giant fennel, the henceforth inextinguishable fire, to which they owed new benefits every day. They learned successively, from that sage beloved of Heaven, all the sciences necessary to the conservation of human beings and their wellbeing.

It was there that Isuren built the first city posterior to the deluge, which, in the name of his son Casyapa,[1] great among all the sons of men, was named Casyapa-Pora; and the land where they settled was called Kachmyr, the land of happiness.

---

1 Casyapa, or Kashyapa, is one of the seven ancient sages of the Rig-Veda and other ancient Sanskrit texts. Some nineteenth-century scholars opined that his name was the origin of the name of the territory of Kashmir, or Kachmyr in Martin's version. In ancient Greek texts referring to Alexander's expedition to India various words similar to Kasyapa-pur appear, including Kaspapyros—employed by the geographer Hecataeus of Miletus—which carried a more explicit link to the Greek word for fire. Hecataeus was the first Greek historian to mention the "Celtic" people, who came to occupy a significant place in Martin's semi-mythical history of Gaul.

From the first families assembled around Isuren a great people was born, which extended throughout Aryavarta,[1] and from there to the rest of the world, but without ever forgetting the mountains from which it obtained its origin. The high places in which the Creator and the created universe had been revealed became, in the traditions of their descendants, the abode of the celestial powers, and the glory of Isuren passed from century to century and from nation to nation, always the same under twenty different names: Osiris in Misraim, Prometheus among the noble Hellenes, and Ebusopas on the banks of the Euxin.[2]

---

1 Aryavarta is a Sanskrit term meaning land of the Aryas, and the origin of much-abused term "Aryan"; it referred to the northern part of the Indian subcontinent.
2 Ebusopas is a name cited in French versions of Pliny's natural history, appropriated by Louis Poinsinet de Sivry (1733-1804) in his primitive anthropological treatise *Origine des premières societés, des sciences, des arts et des idiomes anciens et modernes* (1769), in which work Martin presumably found it, and much of the inspiration for his own hypothetical prehistory.

100

THE MERCHANT OF CAIRO

I

"BY my father's beard," said Hassan-Abou-Khalef, nonchalantly raising his chibouk, blackened by the odorous vapor of delectable Latakia tobacco, to his mouth, "I protest, friends, that there are no djinn!"

"Allah!" exclaimed the scandalized members of the audience, raising their hands toward the sky.

"In truth, I tell you that there are no djinn." And such was the credit of Hassan the Rich, Hassan the Wise, and such was the authority of his word, that no one raised a voice against his or criticized his temerity, except by involuntary murmurs.

Hassan was the most renowned of all the merchants of great Kahira, the most knowledgeable of its doctors. Every spring his right hand launched a ship toward the Oriental Ocean and his left another toward the Mediterranean, and every autumn brought them back laden with the treasures of India or Frangistan.[1] While still young he had traveled himself in more countries than are described by Aboufeda, son of Eyoub,[2] and from his world travels he had brought back the science of the Franks, and combined the knowledge of the Brahmins with that of the Arabs, his ancestors. So the people of the city respected his decision like a fatwa, although the zealous imams sometimes thought that Hassan-Abou-Khalef had learned too much from the infidels.

That evening, in the café in the square of Esbekieh, people were being entertained by the curious observations that the merchant had made in the course of his voyages of the various products of each country. The conversation had fallen on all the creatures of God that populate the surface of the world, progressing from other animals to humans, and it was there that Hassan had audaciously broken

1 Author's reference: "Europe."
2 The intended reference must be the fourteenth-century Kurdish historian and geographer whose name is usually Latinized as Abulfeda, although his father was Malik-ul-Aldal. His *Concise History of Humanity* (c1330) was translated into both English and French.

the scale of beings by denying the existence of those substances of air and fire that crown, it is said, the step superior to ours.

"Believe me," he went on, "if the eccentric spirits of which you speak existed anywhere but in your imaginations, we would have made their acquaintance in some of my distant peregrinations. I've visited the famous rocks of Albours, where Persian tradition lodges their redoubtable diwas; I've pronounced all the evocatory formulae in the subterranean galleries of Dom-Daniel of Tunis; I've penetrated, with Occidental seekers of knowledge whom you mistake for seekers of gold, the magical cellars of the Pyramids, but never, I swear to you, have I heard any other voice than the echo of my footfalls, or seen extending behind me any other shadow than my own. In any case, my good friends, it would be easy for me to demonstrate, by means of the unbreakable laws of physics, that invincible destroyer of human errors, that essences as subtle could not subsist in our gross atmosphere. Those who invented djinn doubtless did not know physics."

"So the prophet didn't know everything in this world and the other?" said a grave mullah, fixing his austere gaze upon the presumptuous physiognomy of the merchant. "The djinn didn't come to salute him while he prayed under the palm tree at daybreak? You're putting in doubt the seventy-second chapter of the Koran!"

"The letter kills and the spirit vivifies, as the worshipers of Issa[1] say. The prophet must have lured vulgar intelligence many a time by means of vulgar allegories; it is the same with djinn, in my view, as the story of the camel and the people of Schédad, son of Ad."[2]

"You're very knowledgeable, Abou-Khalef," retorted the mullah, shaking his head, "but pray to Allah not to become even more so, at your expense!"

The merchant smiled, shook out tranquilly the ashes accumulated in the gold-circled bowl of his chibouk, which he handed to a richly-dressed slave, and went out, his hands plunged gracefully into the folds of his cashmere belt.

"Peace be with you, friends," he said, turning round on the threshold, "and believe, on my word, that there are no djinn!"

---

1 Author's note: "Jesus Christ."

2 Islamic tradition relates that Ad, son of Amalek and grandson of Ham, became a tribal leader in Arabia. His two sons, Schedad and Scheded, built a city in the desert, discovered long after it was supposed to have vanished by an Arab who was searching for his lost camel. Schedad's son Dhohok was reputed to be a magician working in association with Iblis (the Devil).

II

"Do you not have enough treasures, Abou-Khalef? Do you not have enough in your fine palace behind the great mosque, in your summer-houses on the cheerful islands of the Nile, in your vast counters in Suez and Skenderoun[1] and galleries always encumbered with the precious merchandise of the two seas? Or are you so weary of the kisses of your faithful Hodeïda that you need, in order to rejoice your heart, the lascivious dances of the bayaderes of Punjab?"

"I don't care about the daughters of Punjab, and I have not strayed far in my heart from my Hodeïida; but I want to see once again the banks of the river Sind, and double my great wealth by means of a bold enterprise, in order that there should no longer be a single merchant in the lands of Islam richer than me."

"Ah! At least, if it is your pleasure to expose on the tenebrous ocean the products of your labor, don't risk with them a life that is so dear to us; if you have no fear for the husband of Hodeïda, at least think of the father of Khalef—your Khalef, whose first smile

---

1 Author's note: "Alexandria."

swelled your breast with joy, and whom you have not quit since his birth!"

"It's for him that I'm departing, and for the two of you that I'll return; this is the moment when the northern monsoon chases the ships of the Sea of Kolzum toward the Strait of Tears;[1] my Christian pilot is skillful, my vessel built by the constructors of Frangistan is as solid as a granite rock, and the fatal El-Mandeb will lose its name for us. I will return before next year's Ramadan."

"Go, then, since prayers and tears are powerless over your inflexible soul; go, and may the benedictions of the prophet accompany you; but never have blacker presentiments oppressed me at the hour of separation!"

Hassan, rebellious, but not insensible to her plaints, embraced his desolate spouse; he deposited a long kiss of farewell on the forehead of the sleeping infant and then mounted one of his dromedaries in order to go and join the caravan from Kahira to Suez at the Lake of Pilgrims.

He had devoted the greater part of his funds to a colossal and audacious speculation. He had conceived the idea of being the first of

---

1 Author's note: "Bab-el-Mandeb, or the Strait of Tears, is thus named because of the extreme danger that the Arabs attach to the idea of traversing it."

his people to cross the great sea from Egypt to India, and there he proposed to buy the most magnificent and immensely valuable fabrics of Kachmyr, of which he hoped to acquire a monopoly throughout the Ottoman Empire.

The crossing was unusually fortunate; a constantly favorable wind enabled his ship to fly across the Red Sea like a seabird. It passed proudly, all sails deployed, before the port of Djidda, the ultimate point of navigation of the ships of Kahira, and went through the terrible El-Mandeb and the menacing reefs of Périm without an instant of peril; then it went into the limitless waters of the Indian Ocean. His lucky star did not abandon him in the open sea, for a breeze from the land, charges with the perfumes of Yemen, took the vessel in the poop as soon as he had doubled the point of Aden, and the west wind blew constantly for three days and three nights.

"By the prophet's mare, what's this?" cried the owner of the ship. "Dog of a pilot, accursed djaour, have you been sent by Iblis, then, to have us eaten by sharks? You haven't warned us that such reefs existed in these waters!"

The vessel had just experienced a commotion that had shaken its entire carcass, and had then become immobile, as if it had run aground.

"That's impossible," the pilot replied. "We're two hundred miles from any land. Drop the sound!"

The cable of the sound unwound, endlessly . . . there was no sand, nor any bed of shellfish; it was necessary to withdraw it; they had unreeled two hundred brasses without finding the bottom.

"If tradition could be trusted," said Abou-Khalef, "I'd believe that we were dealing with a remora, the little fish that, it's claimed, can stop the heaviest ships. In fact, physics, sufficiently fathomed, perhaps offers a natural explanation of that strange power."

Whatever its origin was, it seemed that the phenomenon would infallibly cause the loss of the ship, for the wind had not stopped with it; on the contrary, it redoubled its violence, and although the sails were furled in great haste, it dislocated the stationary hull in all its joints, and bent the masts, indocile to impulsion. A horrible creaking was heard; the mainmast fell, dragged away with the maintops, cables and rigging; its fall crushed the prow of the ship.

All movement in the air ceased immediately and the vessel, as bare as a pontoon, swayed gently on a sea as flat as the blue mirror of a dormant lake; but a waterway was opened and the keel drank in large draughts a wave that was rising, and which kept rising . . .

Abou-Khalef had an intrepid heart; he did not lament or tremble. Perhaps he could still save, for those awaiting him on the banks of the Nile, both his life and his floating wealth; he put his whole soul into that chance and said: "Let's go!"

They embarked on the frail launch hidden in the flanks of the mortally wounded vessel, and Abou-Khalef, darting one last glance at his fine European brig as the oarsmen drew away from it with a vigorous surge, saw it agitate in turbulent foam, and sink, spinning, as if in the spirals of a gigantic screw.

"What is the nearest land?" asked Abou-Khalef.

"Zocotora,[1] I think," the pilot replied.

"Let's head for Zocotora."

They rowed valiantly toward the south.

The sea was so calm and heavy that their oars scarcely lifted it, and every stroke exhausted their vigorous muscles.

Suddenly, they perceived an object in the distance that dominated the azure plain by virtue of its isolation. It was not a rock, for it approached, growing rapidly, and it was

---

1 The remote island usually known nowadays as Socotra.

definitely coming toward them; their own progress was so slow.

They recognized it as an enormous wave, which was advancing of its own accord, without being impelled by any aerial breath.

Gripped by astonishment, they tried to draw away from its path, to slip to one side, and then the other, but the wave kept coming closer and closer, always heading directly for them.

Abou-Khalef felt his breast rise convulsively, thinking about his wife and child.

However, he thought, *it's doubtless only a kind of waterspout, and physics . . .*

He could not finish; the wave was already covering the launch with its immense shadow. It curved its foamy head over the fragile skiff and collapsed like an avalanche.

III

"Allah be blessed, Abou-Khalef! The fire of Heaven has devoured your storehouses in Skenderoun; the sudden flooding of the Nile has ruined your summer-houses and the emirs of the mountains have irrupted into Suez and pillaged your rich counters, but what does all that matter, and even more? Allah be blessed, since I see you again safe and sound after two months of absence. About-Khalef, friend of my heart . . . but how is it that you're silent? You're pale, Ali Hassan! Oh! Why are those garments in tatters, like those of a poor pilgrim? Where are your companions, Hassan? Where is your beautiful European ship?"

"My companions are in the bellies of the fish of the sea; my gold has gone to pave the ocean bed; the bitter gulf cast me up, dying, on the shores of Zocotora. A Frankish vessel picked me up out of charity and deposited me in the port of Aden, and I've returned on foot across the whole of Arabia, begging for my nourishment among the peoples of Yemen and the Bedouins of the desert. Oh, woe is me, who will not even leave to my son what I received from my father!"

"True wealth is sufficiency, not superabundance, the sage has said. You still have your house in Kahira, its gardens, its slaves and its splendors of every sort. We can still live happily there, Abou-Khalef, and many a bey's son would still envy the son of Hassan."

"Bring me the child," said the merchant, calmed but not consoled.

The caresses of the little Khalef finished clearing his father's brow; he sensed that wisdom had spoken to him through Hodeïda's

mouth. After having relaxed his fatigue-hard-
ened limbs in a long warm bath, he sat down
as before between the mother and son, on the
cushions of the banqueting hall, and resolved,
in spite of the scruples of the pious Hodeïda,
to drown his memories in the wine of Cyprus.

The child, with the avidity of his age, had
thrown himself on a bowl of savorous pilau
rice and had borne his two hands, full of his
booty, to his mouth. Suddenly, he shuddered,
changed color and dissolved in tears.

His parents got up fearfully and ran to him.

"I can't eat," he stammered, sobbing.
"There's something there that rejects the morsels from my mouth, and yet I'm very hungry.

In fact, it was impossible to enable him to
swallow the smallest grain of rice."

The terrified mother prostrated herself,
invoking Allah and his prophet tearfully.

About-Khalef did not think of praying;
during his voyages he had forgotten the five
names, and scarcely performed his ablutions.
He sent for a Frankish physician, for he preferred infidels to men of his own people in all
things.

The physician spoke knowledgeably about
all maladies of the stomach in general, and in
particular about the excessive debilitation that
causes aliments to be rejected via the paths
that have received them; then, when he had

spoken at great length the child said: "I don't
have a stomach ache; it's in my mouth that
the rice can't enter."

The doctor learned over him, made him
stick out his tongue, examined successively
the palate, the glottis, the larynx and the
various organs of mastication and deglutition,
and then shook his head and said, with a pity-
ing smile: "Stupidity! Impossible!"

"See for yourself," said the child, weeping
more forcefully.

"Impossible!" cried the physician, when he
had seen that it was true, and he departed,
shrugging his shoulders.

Abou-Khalif had two mullahs summoned.

"It was written that the morsels could not
enter his mouth," they said. "Allah is great!"

The child suffered for three days; milk,
sorbets and the juice of watermelons, the flesh
of which was pressed to his lips, flowed back,
seething, from his throat.

He died on the third night.

IV

Since the strange catastrophe that had robbed
them of their beloved son, the two spouses
had not savored an instant of repose; each
of them, weary of life on their own behalf,

only existed for the other. The intelligence, so vast and so proud, of the man who could no longer name himself Abou-Khalef[1] was as bleak and desolate as an empty tomb, and his heart, once so full of all human felicities, was only connected to the world by one last single bond.

One day, lying on the balcony shaded by lemon-trees and odorous jasmines, he was gazing sadly, by turns, at the main street, whose double line of tall houses dazzled him with its monotonous whiteness, and his Hodeïda, wandering on the terrace of the palace and making pauses to water each of the flowers that the child she had lost had loved.

Suddenly, advancing along the street, four Bedouins appeared, clad in white burnooses and mounted on black horses. It was a rather strange spectacle, for they appeared to belong to the rebel tribes of the Saïd, and yet they were progressing without anyone thinking of disturbing them, and the crowd opened before them with a sort of stupefaction.

Although the pace of their horses seemed to be leisurely, they were beneath Hodeïda's terrace in an instant. They stopped abruptly,

---

1 Author's note: "The Arabs take the name of their son as other peoples take the name of their father; Abou-Khalef signifies 'the father of Khalef.'"

turning to face the wall. The four horsemen stood up in the saddle; three of them united their extended hands; the fourth, with one bound, was lifted up by the arms of his companions; he brandished his spear, planted it in the wall above his head, and two further leaps carried him from the hands that sustained him on to the shaft of the spear and from the spear on to the terrace. A terrible scream penetrated the depths of Hassan's heart: the scream of Hodeïda, seized by the Bedouins.

The abductor's companion had remained in position, as if to receive his perilous descent, but, disdaining that aid and without the slightest hesitation, he slid down the wall, collected his spear in passing, and found himself back in the saddle, his captive motionless on the saddle-bow before him.

Such had been the rapidity of that singular maneuver that a kind of daze had nailed Hassan to the spot, but the first movement of the horses caused that fascination to vanish.

Yataghan in hand, Hassan launched himself into the street, roaring like a lion. The four Bedouins drew away slowly—very slowly—through the bewildered crowd.

Hassan ran with the speed of a hunting panther. At that moment a powerful bey, followed by a host of his invincible mameluks, appeared some forty paces from the brigands.

"Justice!" cried the merchant. "Justice, glorious sultan, against the kafirs of the desert!"

The Bedouins passed, heads and lances held high, between the triple ranks of the motionless mameluks . . .

Hassan emerged from Kahira after them, without the distance that separated him from them increasing or diminishing by a step.

They took their horses into the Nile directly opposite Giza. Hassan threw himself into the river and emerged, exhausted, on the other bank, while they were still riding at the same pace over the great plain of the Pyramids.

Suddenly, they turned round, and waited for him in silence, fixing their eyes upon him, sparkling with sinister fire. Hodeïda had not uttered a cry or a plaint; she was plunged in a profound slumber, perhaps the most profound.

Hassan was gathering himself like a tiger in order to pounce on the bandits, his saber held horizontally before him, when a burst of strange, superhuman laughter thundered, freezing the blood in his veins.

He was alone in the desert.

He fell on the sand, inanimate, as if thunderstruck.

The scales fell from his eyes too late; he finally realized that the God he had forgotten had forgotten him in his turn in that hour of distress. Alas, what use to him now were the vanities of Europe and sciences foreign to the holy book in which all knowledge good for humans was contained?

Hassan tried to drag himself to the river in order to seek a last refuge there, but he could not, because his strength was exhausted, and he lay down on the sand, hoping to die.

At that moment the sun, red and devoid of radiance, was approaching the terminus of its course and seemed to be suspended like a bloody clock-face on the tip of the great pyramid, the enormous shadow of which covered the solitude in the distance.

The star sank gradually behind the mountain of bricks; at the moment when the upper edge of its disk was about to disappear, a great and lugubrious voice emerged from the profound cavities of the monument and vibrated in space for a long time, as if the celestial clock had chimed some infernal hour while losing itself in the shadow.

Immediately, thick darkness enveloped the whole plain; all objects faded away in a common night; only the pyramid stood out in dark red against the black sky.

A dull roar departed from its base, which opened in order to vomit forth a flamboyant mass, a kind of ardent whirlwind formed of a multitude of multicolored flashes; the fiery cloud snaked into a twisted column, and then, elongating all the way to the summit of the monument, crowned it with a spinning circle, the frightful rapidity of which confounded all the colors of the rainbow in an indescribable mixture; but those gleams were sadder than the shadows that surrounded them; one might have thought that the hues were those of an otherworldly prism.

The mysterious cycle suddenly bounded above the pyramid and, tightening again into a compact mass, plunged through the air like a whirlwind, straight toward the merchant, frozen by amazement.

As they approached, each of the flashes that composed the marvelous assemblage grew, took on form and developed . . .

Hassan soon saw red, green, blue and yellow bodies raising bald and menacing heads, and extending membranous wings . . .

They arrived with a noise like the flight of a thousand eagles, and their dense battalions, circling the unfortunate merchant, clutched one another with the iron claws of their wings, and swayed slowly for a time, dancing.

Their magical dance was bizarre and terrible; their round did not turn with the magical refrains; they bounded in place, launching by turns into Hassan's face their sniggering visages and their clawed feet.

And each one repeated in its turn, while the merchant's eyes were obliged to follow the direction of each voice, one after another:

"Hassan Abou-Khalef, do you believe in djinn?"

"Take him!" cried the great voice that had given the initial signal.

And Hassan, gripped by horror, felt the powerful hand of a djinni set his entire body ablaze . . .

He was borne into space by the wing-beats of his persecutor, while a terrible chant was sometimes drawn out in lamentable howls and sometimes rang in his ears in hoarse bursts.

> It would be better for him had his body
>   remained
> On the battlefield,
> That a daughter of men in her sad entrails
> Had never borne him!
>
> The ghouls of the abyss.
> Awaiting their victim,
> Are hungry.
> Their ardent claws are reaching out,
> Their teeth gnawing in expectation,
> For your bosom.

You have not consulted, before taking
    flight
The tutelary rose;[1]
We, who know your name and your
    mother's[2]
Will tell you your fate.

Amid the winds of flame
Incessantly, your soul

Will burn;
Or, beneath dull fires
In cold caverns
Will tremble . . .

------

1 Author's note: "The rose of Jericho, or of Idumea, curves its branches in the heat; its branches interlace in the form of a globe. It reopens them in damp weather. Before setting forth on a voyage, the people of the region come to consult the rose-bushes. If they close their branches, the enterprise is regarded as desperate; if they open them, success is supposedly certain." Idumea is an ancient Greek term for Edom, an ancient kingdom the territory of which is now mostly in Jordan.

2 Author's note: "By means of Rami science, someone's destiny can be predicted, provided that he gives his name and that of his mother." The common Arabic name Rami is usually said to mean "loving" but it appears to be derived from a verb whose meanings include "to indicate."

"Silence!" cried the voice, again.

Hassan was deposited on the platform of the pyramid. He raised his wild eyes; it was the king of the djinn, the formidable djinn, at whose feet he had been thrown.

Around him, above his head, soared the redoubtable powers of djinnistan; below him plunged the eight faces of the pyramid, at the angles of which black afrits were suspended like gigantic bats, while, the savage and cruel spirits that inhabit ruins, sterile rocks and the dust of tombs were crawling on the slopes like filthy reptiles. And all their ironic and blazing gazes, converging on his, were burning his terrified eyes.

"People of the invisible regions," said the voice of the king of the spirits, "what shall we do with this son of Adam that Allah has abandoned to us?"

"Master," replied an Afrit, raising toward him its red eye and his blue eye, "give him to me so that I can make a present of him to Iblis, my great friend; it will be a great joy for him to put a living man into his inferno."

And it was already extending a flexible trunk to seize its prey.

"Master," howled a ghoul, slithering like a snake over the oblique surface of the mon-ument, "my children are hungry for living human flesh; they have only eaten dead flesh for a fortnight."

And its monstrous head was already opening a tooth-filled maw behind the victim.

"Master, master," roared, hissed and mewled the kothrobs, djeheims and all the subaltern evil spirits ground beneath the redoubtable Sanhedrin,[1] "Give him to us, give him to us, so that we can make charms with his bones, charms with his marrow and charms with his grease."

And all of them rushed insolently around the judge and the guilty man, and a thousand hooked hands, curved over the unfortunate merchant with a horrible, extraordinary tumult.

"Rabble!" cried the angry monarch. "None of you . . ."

The resonance of that terrible voice was such that the entire avid crowd precipitated from the height of the pyramid like rocks tumbled down a mountain by an earthquake.

Hassan also fell into the void, simultaneously losing his breath and the sentiment of his existence . . .

---

1 The terms *kothrob* and *djehein* are idiosyncratic, but the reference to the Sanhedrin implies that they are categories of the djinn supposed by legend to have been imprisoned by Solomon.

Suddenly, he uttered a profound sigh and opened his eyes. He thought that he was raising them on another world, but he recognized once again the land of Misraim!

He was lying on the bank of the Nile; the stars were shining in the sky; silence reigned over the plain, and next to the merchant, on the river bank, a European brig was moored.

Hassan looked at the vessel; it was his.

He launched himself on to the deck; everyone was asleep, master, pilot and sailors. Two other individuals were also asleep under a silken tent at the stern of the vessel.

They were his wife and his son!

On the mainmast shone, in luminous characters, these sentences from the *Garden of Wisdom*:[1]

The man who seeks wisdom is a sage; the man who thinks he has found it is a madman.

Never speak about that which you do not know, and doubt that which you do.

---

1 The reference is to a collection of aphorisms known by various titles associated with the mystical form of Islam known as Sufism.

AN ADVENTURE OF THE ABBÉ DE GONDY[1]

"WHAT I deem to be most worthy of remark in your life," said Madame de Sévigné, "and what I admire most in you, my dear cardinal, the interests of God apart, is the incomparable skill with which you can

---

1 Jean-François-Paul de Gondi (1613-1679), Cardinal de Retz, was a leading agitator in the conspiracy known as the Fronde, which precipitated civil war in France and nearly undermined the Bourbon monarchy, important by virtue of his position as Archbishop of Paris. He left behind a memoir of his turbulent, distinctly unholy and rather puzzling life, which was severely censored when initially published in 1717, and only properly restored in 1836, after the present story was published, although Martin might well have read the unexpurgated version before its publication. The addressee of the memoirs is unknown, although many people assumed that it was the Marquise de Sévigné (1626-1696), his relative by marriage, with whom the cardinal corresponded late in life, and whose belatedly-published letters provided another important memoir of her era,.

124

tackle affairs and gallantry head on, without allowing the latter to thrive at the expense of others nor ever allowing the influence of the petticoat—which is even more marvelous—to direct your politics . . ."

"You're forgetting, it seems to me, Mademoiselle de Chevreuse," the beautiful Duchesse de Montausier interjected.[1]

"It's not forgetfulness on my part," said Madame de Sevigné, "but that passion served the dear cardinal's designs so well that one cannot say, in truth, whether interest guided their amorous liaison or amour their liaison of interest. In either case, you'll grant me, I think that a courtier more devoted to ladies was less governed by ladies; one could remove from his history his innumerable amours without

---

1 "Mademoiselle de Chevreuse" was Charlotte-Marie de Lorraine (1627-52), the daughter of Marie-Aimée de Rohan; the latter was banished from the French court after allegedly engaging the pregnant queen in games that caused her to miscarry, and she spent the rest of her life engaging with her daughter in conspiracies against the crown, including the Fronde, Charlotte-Marie, who never married, was widely alleged to be the Cardinal de Retz's mistress. The original has "Duchesse de Montansier," and repeats the error, but the intended reference must be to the Duchesse de Montausier, alias "la belle Julie," featured subsequently in one of the author's own footnotes. Perhaps the typeaetter could not read Martin's handwriting.

taking with them the cause or the mechanism of a single one of his actions or projects during the civil war."

"I'm very grateful," put in Cardinal de Retz, "for the favorable opinion that you want to manifest regarding your unworthy servant; but after undertaking my confession, I believe that I would remain in mortal sin if I concealed something from you for reasons of false glory. You think, Mesdames, that all my determinations of any importance were taken outside my relations with your sex. You will therefore not be slightly surprised if I tell you that a sidelong glance imprudently directed into a mirror decided my entire existence, that the glance in question made me cardinal Archbishop of Paris, and that but for that glance I would be, like so many other ducs, a marquis or something similar, consuming my wealth between a wife and child in the depths of an old manor in Anjou, not to say Poitou, and knowing nothing of barricades but those of the late Monsieur de Guise-le-Balafré[1] of turbulent memory."

"A sly glance! Bah! So many of them have been lent to you!" exclaimed Madame de Sévigné.

---

1 Henri I, Duc de Guise, nicknamed "le Balafré" [i.e, Scarface], a key figure in the sixteenth-century French Wars of Religion.

"It's not a joke, God's truth!"

"In that case, tell us about it, quickly. I'm already almost dying of impatience to hear your story; if I perish without confession before you begin, I put my soul on your conscience."

"It's not for fear of such a slight burden, but in order not to see the end of such a beautiful life, that I'm obeying in all haste.

"You know well enough by virtue of what entire and absolute determination I was thrown into a profession for which Heaven had certainly not shaped me. You knew my father, the Comte de Joigny, his inflexible character and his austere piety. His ardent zeal for my salvation—stimulated, it's true, albeit unknown to him, by his predilection for my older brother and the idea of conserving within the family the diocese of Paris—under the pretext of avoiding worldly temptations for me, constituted within me the permanence of sacrilege by attaching to the Church the least ecclesiastical soul in the universe.

"In any case, his intention was good, if scantly appropriate; for that reason, God grant him peace and mercy!

"I was twenty years old and not yet irrevocably engaged in holy orders, although already promised to the Abbeys of Buzay, Quimerlay and La Chamur, when my father obtained for his beloved son the hand of the eldest daughter of Monsieur le Duc de Retz, then the head of our family. Our relative having no male heir, that brilliant union transported into our branch of the family the honors of the dukedom, and fulfilled my father's wishes.

"I do not know from where a sudden desire came time to witness the happiness of a brother who had never been anything, at the most, but indifferent for me. Was it the scant disposition that I believed I saw in my father to take me to the wedding, or a vague thought relative to what I had to say to one of Mademoiselle de Retz's younger sisters? I can be certain of nothing today. Nevertheless, I acted some time in advance in a fashion to get into my father's good graces again. I pretended to be touched by a devotion entirely new for me; I made a retreat for a week in order to compile a commentary on Saint Basile and Saint Augustine; in brief. I played my part to the edification of my family, with the result that I made the journey, for which I carefully refrained from testifying the slightest desire.

"We arrived early in the morning at the Château de Beaupré, where the marriage was to be celebrated. Faithful to the spirit of my role, I masked with a perfect indifference my keen desire to be introduced to the ladies, and without waiting for them to get up, as my brother did, I bravely retired to my chamber with a large book of hours under my arm.

"Once the door had closed on the two of us, you can imagine that the breviary and I were immediately divorced, it to display in vain on a dresser its belly gaping after a reader's eye, me to plant myself in ambush behind the large curtain that covered my window—for I had decided heroically to wait for dinner time before putting in an appearance.

"I was not lying in wait for long before hearing a glazed door open almost facing me; two people advanced on to the balcony to which that casement opened. It was my brother Pierre, accompanied by a very gracious demoiselle, with whom he seemed to be engaged in gallant conversation.

"It would be difficult to express the effect that the ideas of my future sister-in-law had on me, succeeding the first glance that I cast upon her; there was a combat of a thousand confused sentiments, from which I could only disentangle one at first: I would have preferred her not to be my sister-in-law! I would have liked not to ask anything further of myself, but I understood only too quickly all the rest.

"I had just received the most profound shock that my heart, too vulnerable to impressions of that sort, had ever endured. It was a sweet, penetrating emotion, almost disengaged from the senses, the existence of which my first intrigues had never revealed; my arrogant and mocking humor and my conquering pride, were so far from it that my heart swelled and I felt my eyes filling with tears.

"I was already too much of a rake not to blush at the simplicity of that child; I scarcely believed in 'secret knots' or 'sympathies' and I directed a formal attack against myself, admonishing myself for the damage I would do to my good renown if Attichy and the Marquis de Poissy found out that I had wept amorously over my sister-in-law.

"Those powerful considerations had no effect; Mademoiselle de Retz's retreat did not lead to that of the thoughts that she had awakened in my soul, and when the dinner bell rang I was still lying down, my eyes in my fists, alternately raging against myself or ceding without resistance to the current of my *imaginations*.

"When I went into the great hall, the first thing that struck my gaze was the demoiselle from before conversing with my father and my brother. I leaned against the paneling, because I thought that my legs were about to refuse to sustain me; however, my strength of mind and, above all, the fear that people might notice something extraordinary in me, soon rendered my self-control. Lowering my eyes without affectation, I was advancing slowly to compliment my amiable relative when Madame la Duchesse de Retz, whom I already knew for having seen her in the home of my uncle, the Archbishop of Paris, appeared, with another young lady, whose beauty, less touching but more delicate than the first, was heightened by everything that a splendid adornment can add to the attractions of the most beautiful woman.

"'Monsieur l'Abbé,' said my father, designating the newcomer to me, 'come here and salute your sister-in-law.'

"That was, I believe, the first time in my life that I obeyed a paternal injunction gladly . . . gladly, as I say, but not with great celerity, it's true, for that would have been impossible for me, shock and joy having taken away the use of my legs in their turn.

"A second 'Come here, then!' returned it to me. I acquitted my duty briefly; then, as the signal had been given to go to table, I made a half-turn, *by chance*, beside my beauty. Palluau, whom you have encountered in society under the name of Maréchal de Clérambault,[1] was disposed, without fear of competition, to offer her his hand when I found myself between them, and the demoiselle's hand in mine, all, without any doubt, as innocently as anything in the world.

"It seemed that my strength was exhausted by that triumph, because I remained sitting next to her for some time without speaking to her or looking at her.

"'I thought I had to felicitate in you a sister,' I finally said, in a low voice. 'Thanks be rendered to Heave that I was mistaken.'

"'The compliment is more civil for Louise than for me!' she replied, raising toward me eyes of an extreme softness, albeit expressing a little astonishment; but she veiled them immediately with her long eyelids, but the gaze that had met hers permitted no mistake as to the meaning of my words.

"I dared not converse in a slightly vivid fashion on that occasion; too many enemy sentinels might signal all our movements, and it was necessary not to risk shipwreck while putting to sea, but I knew full well that I was well and truly caught and that I had

____

1 Philippe de Clérambault de La Palluau (1606-1665), a career soldier who rose to be a Maréchal de France.

never loved anyone before Mademoiselle de Scépeaux—that was the name given by the family to the second daughter of Monsieur le Duc de Retz. In pledging my faith to her internally, with a thousand oaths, I swear to you that the duchy of Beaupréau, which was to revert to her one day, accompanied by an income of eighty thousand livres, was very far from my mind, although before the voyage I might perhaps have built more than one vague chimera on that basis . . ."

"Come on, come on, Cardinal, confess that it didn't spoil anything," interjected Madame de Sevigné, "and don't be ungrateful to the goodness of God!"

"I have nothing to confess; it's enough to speak ill of oneself without being obliged to calumny."

"Was she very pretty, then?" asked Madame de Montausier. "Brunette or blonde? Lively or languid?"

"She was a mixture of all that is most delightful in both: a complexion similar in splendor to the most brilliant flowers in Julie's garland," he added, smiling, "eyes and a mouth like those of Mademoiselle de la Roche-Couart,[1] with a touching and modest

1 The author adds footnotes to this paragraph to explain that "the famous collection entitled *Guirlande-*

languor that the latter will never have in her life; and under all those external graces the most natural charm, the most loving and most sincere soul. Poor Marie!

"The next day, as I was walking in the garden, dreaming about the means of obtaining a conversation with her, I found her sitting under a hornbeam. Her forehead was inclined over her hand, her beautiful brown curls floating in the wind over her snow-white neck.

"She lifted her head at the sound of my footsteps, blushed, and tried to withdraw.

"'Am I so odious to you, then, that my mere presence forces you to flee?' I exclaimed, dolorously.

"She stayed.

"We maintained silence for some time. 'Why then have you quit the company and the proximity of my mother,' she said, finally, in the distracted tone that releases words at hazard when the thoughts are elsewhere.

---

de-Julie was offered to Julie d'Angennes by the Duc de Montausier, her lover, and subsequently her husband" and that Mademoiselle de la Roche-Court subsequently became Madame de Montespan, Louis XIV's most famous official mistress. The manuscript in question was composed by several habitués of the famous Hôtel de Rambouillet, including the then-Marquis de Montausier, and presented to Julie d'Angennes on her birthday in 1641.

"'There were too many people there—or too few.'

"A deeper crimson colored her cheeks. 'And then,' I continued, gazing with a somber expression at my black soutane, 'this shroud that envelops me while alive weighs upon me amid the joys of others like a leaden cloak; it stifles me . . .'

"'Everything that is reported about your aversion for the clergy and the violence that has been done to you is true, then? Poor cousin, when others criticize your obstinacy and your folly before me, when they envy that golden miter of which, they say, you do not know the full value, I understand you and I sympathize with your efforts, and your torment . . .'

"'Oh, Marie, Marie, is it possible? What torments would not be forgotten for one of your tears? And yet, what you say is true, I have suffered a great deal. Elder children are fortunate, in truth. And yet, has not God made us as human as them? Do we not have the same heart and the same passions? Do we not need happiness too? But may I be accursed if I yield like a coward to the destiny that is imposed on me!"

"'Alas, our fortunes are similar. They want to punish me, too, with the convent, for the crime of not being born first.'

"'You! You, snatched from this world, of which you make the most precious charm! Buried in a monastic sepulcher! The barbarians! Never! Marie,' I cried, throwing myself at her feet, 'Marie, I love you! I will extract you from that life of ennuis and miseries! Come, flee your tyrants with me!'

"She recoiled from my impetuous transports. 'What are you daring to say?' she stammered, her eyes moistened by tears. 'Is it recognizing my confidence to insult me thus?'

"'Insult you! Oh, Marie . . . Marie, our two existences are in your hands,' I added, rapidly, lowering my voice. 'We shall see one another again!'

"And I concealed myself hastily behind a yew bush, because I had heard the footsteps of several strollers a short distance away.

"The eve of the wedding arrived without my being able to see her again in private; one might have thought that a malign demon was thwarting all my attempts and taking pleasure in undoing the best laid plans at the very moment of success. I was desperate; the hours and the days went by at a frightful speed, and every minute lost might be irreparable!

"While I abandoned myself to those anxious reflections, I suddenly encountered an aged chambermaid, who had brought

Marie up and by whom she was loved dearly. The dread of misplacing my confidence in an affair of such importance had made me hesitate until then to open up to that woman, but I could not delay any longer and I broached the matter frankly, begging the woman to procure me a conversation with Marie, promising her mountains of gold if she consented to serve me.

"'I don't want your promises,' the good woman replied, looking me in the eyes. 'For what do you take me?'

"'For Marie's best, or rather only, friend. I wouldn't have declared myself to you otherwise.'

"'The old woman made me take Our Lord and the Holy Virgin as witnesses to my matrimonial intentions, and notified me that, since I was an honest fellow, it would be a great joy to aid me in extracting her dear child from that house of Satan; 'for,' she added, 'the poor child was no better accommodated there, not to mention what was reserved for her in the future.'

"In brief, she took me up to her room, and half an hour later I saw Marie come in, who shivered and uttered a cry on seeing me, for the old woman had not informed her of the reason for which she had been invited, thinking judiciously that it was up to me to give her suitable explanations in that regard.

"'You here!' cried Marie, on seeing me at her knees. 'It's unworthy! Leave me, Monsieur! To use such a subterfuge . . .'

"'I had no choice! Forgive me, Marie, but this isn't the time to listen to vain scruples! Answer me, oh, deign to answer me: do you want my heart, my hand, my entire life? Do you hate me enough to prefer the convent to me? You have only to choose between the two of us. Tell me, Marie, could you love me? Perhaps we have only this hour to determine our double future forever. If a word is too much, let a glance or a nod of the head express that sweet confession! You consent, don't you, that I save you from the long dolors of the cloister, that on my own account I escape for you an insupportable yoke? I have striven to render myself incapable of those detested vows by risking my life in incessantly renascent duels; will you refuse me a gentler means of avoiding them?'

"'No more duels, then,' she finally replied, gazing at me with a ravishing expression.

"I burned her hands with my kisses. 'Oh, no, never!—for my days are no longer my own! You'll go with me, then? You'll go abroad with your husband. You'll admit all the measures that I shall have to take?'

"'It's necessary,' she replied.

"I emerged from that interview drunk on hope and sure of my happiness. Adieu ambition and glory, the life of a speech-maker conspirator, the object of all my youthful dreams! Adieu Fiesque, Rienzi, Catalina! A placid and fortunate life, an old château on the cheerful banks of the Loire, and Marie: such would henceforth be my horizon, my goal, my career!

"*Heu! ludibria ventis!*—or, if you prefer it, Mesdames, man proposes and God disposes . . .

"The day after the wedding, the entire company was to take the road to Machecoul. I was delighted with that expedition; Machecoul is only a league from the sea!

"I departed immediately in order to go an affirm my Abbaye de Buzay, situated five leagues from Machecoul; I withdrew four thousand écus in cash, with a part of which I made sure that the captain of a Dutch ship would be in the harbor at Retz; then I returned triumphantly to join my beauty.

"For the sake of prudence, I did not seek a private conversation with her; I had our confidante give her a note in which I informed her that I would wait for her on the shore at sunrise the day after tomorrow, and that we would set sail for Holland with amour for a pilot.

"When I presented myself that evening in Madame de Retz's room, Marie whispered three words into my ear in a low but firm voice: 'I'll be there.'

"I dared not thank her by means of a gaze imprinted with all my gratitude; I trembled that others might encounter it in passing.

"A mirror placed at the back of the room was our common interpreter.

"I was behind Marie, and I saw, reproduced faithfully in the polished mirror, all the emotions of her mobile and gracious visage. She could also see my image, and was smiling at it most delectably, while her blue eyes faded with an intoxicating languor.

"No moment of my stormy career has made me forget that one, not even the glorious day when Paris, alternately appeased and roused by my voice, blockaded the queen and the fearful Mazarin in the Palais-Royal.

"Alas, there were two of us at the focal point of the mirror. The other was Palluau, a great friend of my sister-in-law, whose devoted chevalier he had been long before her marriage. My sister-in-law was for Marie what my brother was for me!

"The next day, the first words that my brother addressed to me were an order to make my adieux to the ladies, because the *ordinaire* of Paris had brought the most urgent news and it was necessary for us to go to Nantes that evening.

"Astounded as I was by that blow, I was so sure that I had not committed any imprudence that I did not think of a discovery.

"All was not lost so long as that was the case. I let myself be taken away with a good grace, but that night, I took my time so well that I escaped, unknown to everyone. I mounted a horse and, after crossing the Loire. I ran flat out all the way to Machecoul, where I arrived before dawn.

"First light showed me Captain Van-Ost's ship bobbling on the paling sea, but no one on the shore, where the fishermen of the Retz coast were busy putting their boats, run aground on the sand, back into the water.

"The sun rose and climbed over the horizon. Nothing! I waited, and waited. All my blood was seething in my veins; at every instant I thought I perceived horsemen riding from Nantes in search of me. I wandered, drawing my horse after me, still fuming from its race, biting my gloves with rage and digging my spurs into the sand.

"The poor captain exhausted himself in futile signals.

"Finally, I saw a woman's mantle floating in the distance; I responded with a piercing cry to the old mariner's loud-hailer and, leaping into the saddle, I flew toward my promise.

"By all the demons of Hell! It was only the old chambermaid.

"'Where is your mistress?' I cried, in an unintelligible voice.

"'God knows, my dear monsieur!' the old woman replied, weeping. 'Madame her mother made her climb into a closed carriage with her this morning, and they went away without saying anything to anyone. It's not the fault of the poor child, at least, for she was weeping piteously when she was forced to enter the vehicle . . .'

"All was known, there was no more doubt! And they had found nothing surer to frustrate our plans than to accelerate the one long made to put her into religion.

"I was tempted momentarily to urge my horse into the sea until the waves swallowed us both. Reflection stopped me; only the will of our parents was still between us; divine and human laws had not yet separated us irrevocably, and I might yet recover her . . .

"I returned to Nantes; no one asked me any question regarding my absence, but two days later I perceived that my purse had disappeared. It contained, in addition to my four thousand écus, the monuments of my first gallantries—a loss that scarcely worried me, for those objects had been effaced from my memory.

"On my return to Paris my first concern was, of course, to discover Marie's retreat; but I employed in vain all the facilities that my position in the clergy gave me in that regard, and in vain I sent adroit and faithful agents on campaign; it was more than six months before I obtained the slightest enlightenment regarding the fate of my poor cousin.

"It was the greatest hazard in the world that put me on the track; one of my valets de chambre, whom I had dispatched to the south of France in search of new information, being in Grenoble, had taken it into his head to pass to the other side of the mountains in order to visit relatives he had in Chambéry.

"The man in question had a keen passion and a great deal of aptitude for vocal music. Having entered into the church of a convent at the hour of vespers, he stopped to listen to the nuns' chants, and was singularly struck by the voice of one of them, which combined with the clearest and most brilliant notes of all of them a plenitude and profundity very rare in a woman.

"A strange memory crossed his mind; he had once admired in Mademoiselle de Scépeaux, whom he had heard singing two or three times, the same faculty that he rediscovered at that moment in the depths of the Savoie; only the voice that he had just heard made the most intimate fibers vibrate in the hearts of those who heard it, by virtue of the profound and inexpressible sadness hidden in the depths of all its tones.

"Our man wanted to put his conscience in repose; he made the acquaintance of the gardener, questioned the nun in charge of the convent door, and did it so skillfully that he discovered that the singer was a Frenchwoman of distinction, although no one could tell him the name of her family or what had brought her to the convent, suffering extremely and very depressed, six months before.

"Ten days later my faithful emissary was in Paris, and a week after that I was in Grenoble, where I awaited the response to a letter that I had charged my man with getting to Marie.

"Everything was ready. I had no doubt of success. Hidden in a village in the mountains, I was to cross them as soon as I had received Marie's consent. To abduct her and flee with her to Geneva would then by easy for me.

Once there, we would brave our tyrants in peace.

"One morning, while I was calculating for the hundredth time the number of hours that my messenger would require to return to me, my host introduced a courier who had been sent to me from Chambéry. It was not my man, and the letter was not from Marie.

It was from the abbess of the convent, and informed me that the noble demoiselle to whom I judged it appropriate to address my proposals of marriage in such a roundabout fashion, had been for a month, thanks to the dispensations of Monseigneur the bishop of Chambéry, one of the brides of Our Lord.

"'She a nun and me a priest!' I cried, seizing a pistol hidden in my doublet. I held it to my temple for a long time, my finger posed on the trigger . . .'

"But you didn't press it," said Madame de Sévigné.

"No. I threw the weapon down at my feet, after one of those meditations that age a man by ten years in a few minutes. 'A priest!' I said, with a convulsive laugh. 'Why not? Cardinal de Richelieu is a priest too!'

"I have never known by what means Marie's consent was obtained. Some of those

letters from women that I mentioned bore
no date; she might have been persuaded to
believe in my infidelity.

"I have never had any news of her since.

"You can see. Mesdames, that a single
sidelong glance determined my entire existence . . ."

THE JARL'S DAUGHTER
A Norse Saga

I

BRUNHILDE, the daughter of the chief, is sitting next to a window in the banqueting hall awaiting her father's return, and looking into the distance in the valley to discover Snorro's hunt

The cheeks of the brunette girl have lost their crimson tint, and her blue eyes are veiled by a cloud, like those of an Elfe to whom the powers of Walhalla have revealed dire things. She is thinking about the words of Jarl Snorro, and her father's solemn voice is still vibrating in her ears.

"By Freya the great, to whom you were consecrated, you shall not be the wife of a foreigner worshiping a foreign god; no warrior will take the shield-maiden away on his ship unless he professes or adopts the religion of the brave!"

Alas, Siegmar the Teuton is a Christian, and the worshipers of Christ, it is said, would renounce happiness and life rather than their God. In any case, is not Siegmar's will as iron as that of Snorro? Brunhilde cannot hope to bend either one of those inflexible souls, and yet her heart cannot be detached from Siegmar the Teuton.

The evening mist is descending over the hills in black shade; the extremities of the valley resound with marking and whinnying.

"Throw another entire tree on the ardent fire! Fill from the casks the pitchers of beer, hydromel and whisky; for here come our hunters bringing back game for the evening meal."

Brunhilde's bosom swelled under her fur-lined coat; she shivered on seeing Siegmar riding to her father's right.

"Come on, Brunhilde the black-haired; get up to honor the king of the feast. By my good ship, there are rude companions in the German lands, and Siegmar has conducted himself as a true Norseman would have done; he was the one who challenged the bear, face to face, breast to breast, and disemboweled it loyally with his knife. Hurrah for Siegmar the German!"

They entered the banqueting hall joyfully, and Brunhilde's soul was light and glad, because Snorro the Old had praised her young hero.

A noisy gaiety expanded the faces of the guests during the long meal; the fraternity of the hunt is paramount for the men of the North, after that of the battlefield.

When Siegmar had emptied several times over the horn circulating from hand to hand, full to the circlet of gold that crowns its orifice, the fermented beverage warmed his breast and rendered his tongue bolder. He struck the table with his robust fist in order to demand silence.

"Listen to me Snorro, noble Jarl! I have five hundred warhorses in my meadows in Lauenburg, five hundred men-at-arms and twice as many archers ready to march when I deploy my war pennons. I have my vote in the imperial election; what is worth even more, I have the blood of Witikind[1] in my veins. Do

1 Witikind, Wittekind or Widukind, was a Saxon chief who became a significant opponent of the Frankish king who eventually became known as Charlemagne during a tribal war fought between 775 and 785; the Franks massacred thousand of Saxons, and the survivors, including Witikind, were forced to convert

you believe that the mingling of that blood can be a dishonor to a king of the sea? Snorro the Old, it is necessary that you give me your daughter, who has given me her love!"

Brunhilde went as pale as if life had suddenly abandoned her beautiful body.

The Jarl kept silent for a moment; his lowered eyes and his motionless face did not betray his thought.

"The blood of Witikind reddens your veins," he said, finally, in an imposing voice. "It is true, and by virtue of that, I would like to ignore the fact that your race has not followed the ways of Witikind, in accepting the servitude of Romans. Listen in your turn; do right to my request, and I will do right to yours." He lifted the horn full of strong beer. "Siegmar of Lauenburg, this is my toast: praise to the sons of Odin, the god of free men! Malediction upon the sectators of Christ, the god of slaves! Do likewise!"

Siegmat stood up, is teeth clenched and his eyes shining with a somber fire.

"Well, will you repeat after me: Malediction upon the belief of the Romans?"

---

to Christianity—although Christian legend naturally offers a different account. Martin could not know that in the twentieth century Widukind would be idolized by German nationalists, especially the Nazis.

The fumes of whisky and those of anger rose together to the Teuton's brain.

"Shut up, blasphemer!" he cried. "Christ is the unique son of the omnipotent Father, and Thor and Odin are dogs!"

"Hella[1] has heard you!" roared the Jarl, and leapt upon him, knife in hand.

Twenty poniards were around the Teuton, who was backed up against the wall, brandishing his broadsword.

Snorro's daughter threw herself between the naked blades.

"Stop!" she cried, in a resounding voice. "You shall only reach the breast of the German through that of a shield-may! Stop, for the foreign guest is sacred, and woe betide whoever takes his life for words escaped during the cup of a feast!"

Her long black hair floated in disorder over her swan-like neck; her pupils were resplendent and her forehead seemed radiant with divine light. The warriors thought they were seeing a Valkyrie, and lowered their bloodthirsty daggers.

"Let him depart, then," said Snorro, looking at her grimly. Let him return to his native land safe and sound! But I swear to all the gods that if the sun finds him in our Danish

____

1 Author's note: "The goddess of death."

marches tomorrow the crows will dine on his corpse."

"It is not your pardon or your safe conduct that I accept, Snorro, but I shall go because I do not want it to be necessary, between her lover and her husband, for Brunhilde to have to weep for a dead man and hate a survivor, Adieu, then, since you have wished it, Jarl Snorro!"

II

"Someone fetch Brunhilde," said the chief, with an anxious expression. "I had bad dreams last night, and I want her to sing on her harp the stories of the Edda, to expel the black humor from my soul."

"Jarl," said the servants, "Brunhilde is not in this abode. We have searched for her, but she has not shown herself to us; we have called out, but she has not replied."

The chief went up on to the platform of his tower and plunged his eagle gaze into the valley, but the mist enveloped it like a mantle in its obscure pleats.

He called with his powerful voice: "Brun-hilde!"

Only the crows responded, flying away from the crowns of the fir-trees in fear.

The only warrior uttered a dull groan, and his gray hair bristled over his forehead, as if Loki, the god of mischief, had pressed it with his burning hand.

When he had descended from the tower, his faithful followers surrounded him, their eyes anxious and their ears attentive.

"Mount up!" he cried.

That was the entire allocution of Brunhil-de's father.

And they departed. They passed like a hurricane over the heathlands, always flying as straight as a bolt from an arbalest, climbing steep slopes at a gallop, leaping profound crevasses in the granitic rocks.

They finally stopped their chargers covered with bloody foam at the foot of a sheer mountain, and climbed rapidly to the summit.

From there, their gaze scanned the distant waves of the petty bight and its lacy islets, wild coasts of Jutland, and their bays and profound inlets.

A stifled exclamation died in Snorro's throat; his arm extended as if to curse showed them, almost beneath them, a boat moored in a little creek off the shore.

Two figures, one of them recognizable as a woman by her loose vestments, were twenty paces from the boat.

Snorro uttered a cry so terrible that the two lovers heard it and raised their heads toward the summit of the mountain.

The fugitive shuddered, fell to her knees, and extended her suppliant hands toward the chief. Her companion lifted her in his arms, carried her to the boat, and severed the moorings with a blow of his ax.

The frail craft bounded on the turbulent black waves.

Snorro darted a despairing glance around him; then his eyes flashed like lightning in the dark clouds of a storm. He had recognized his almadie[1] at anchor in a neighboring inlet.

"To sea!" he cried.

The old pirate Haldan, his companion during thirty years of war, shook his head as he looked at the squall that was rising with the east wind on the coasts of Seeland. Then he repeated, like the others: "To sea!"

----

1 The French term *almadie* appears to have been invented in the sixteenth century to describe various kinds of bark or dug-out canoes; it is unusual to find it applied to a Norse "serpent ship."

For some time Snorro had remained as somber as a phantom emerged from its tumulary mound, but when he had perceived the boat in the distance deploying its white sail, he recovered all the impetuous energy that the unexpected coup had suppressed in him. He leaned over the prow of the ship as if he were able to imprint a more rapid impulsion on it.

"Hurrah, my good vessel, my serpent of the sea! You have borne your master to victory twenty times over; twenty times you have saved him, wounded, from the fury of the enemy! Today he has been wounded again, but in the heart, and it is not his salvation but his vengeance that he entrusts to you. Hurrah, my faithful followers; we have forty oars against four, and our sail catches ten times as much wind as theirs!"

The distant squall had become a black curtain extended over the vault of the sky; the swell was increasing and roaring endlessly; the sea was seething over the tips of the reefs, which ordinarily surpassed its surface.

To see the fragile craft gliding by turns over the profound slopes of the waves and leaping all the way to the crests of their foaming swirls, one might have thought it a flying fish trying to evade the pursuit of a dorado by means of its aerial bounds.

An immense lightning flash tore the heavy clouds, and the bursts of thunder were confounded with the rumbling of the waves.

"Do you hear, ingrate daughter?" cried the chief. "Thor is threatening you with the voice of his thunder!"

His ship, as light and powerful as a sea-eagle, flew straight toward its goal through the humid mountains that it cut through with its spur.

The almadie dominated the tempest; the feeble boat was dominated by it, and, its sail furled, it allowed itself to be tossed by the caprice of the waves.

Another gust of wind brought its enemy almost upon it.

"Surrender, traitors!" cried Snorro.

"Forgive us, Father!" replied the piercing voice of Brunhilde. "Grant me to the Teuton!"

"Never!"

She embraced the Christian warrior, and, raising to the heavens her face bathed by the marine waves, said: "We shall die together then, my Siegmar!"

Snorro raised his battle-ax, but he did not hurl it at the Teuton, for Brunhilde was suspended from his neck, and the Jarl did not have the heart to kill his daughter.

The ax whistled, however, and, traversing the narrow gap that separated the two vessels, it went to break the boat's yard-arm.

At that moment a typhoon enveloped them and caused them both to spin between the turbulent waves.

Snorro reopened his eyes, blinded by the sea-spray, and saw the smaller boat floating three casts of a javelin away. The almadie exerted the force of its oars to reach the smaller vessel but the waves—was it pity or anger?—hid the boat from the old chief again. A flash of lightning showed it to him almost buried in a furrow in the waves. Then the slope of that profound and mobile path collapsed with a great noise and covered the unfortunate craft.

Snorro felt his heart constricted in an iron grip.

He saw the boat again, closer. Two of the oarsmen had been swept away by the furious wave, but the two lovers were still hugging the remains of the mast. And amid the howls of the torment, a shrill plaint arrived as far as Snorro:

"Pity! Pity, O my father!"

The Jarl's companions relaxed on their oars for a moment, their eyes fixed on the grim visage of their chief; for strange combats were passing in Snorro's soul.

The hurricane that crushes a bush in passing is a terrible thing when it struggles with a mighty oak.

Suddenly, the Jarl raised his head, which was sagging on his bosom, and he lifted the trumpet suspended from his belt to his mouth.

"Come back, come back, Brunhilde! Come back, my daughter! I forgive you! I forgive the Teuton, Brunhilde! Oh, Brunhilde!"

The young woman heard those words of mercy, for she was leaning over the edge of the boat, her arm extended toward her father. If the Jarl had been by their side, he would have seen a tear roll between the lashes of the indomitable Siegmar.

Then the Christian and the virgin took the oars of the two sailors who had been swept into the sea and the boat attempted efforts no less extraordinary to rejoin the vessel that it had previously been fleeing.

They came closer several times, so close that nearly suffered an impact in which the stronger would have smashed the weaker into pieces. Always, though, the waves drew them apart violently at the moment when the Jarl was about to hurl a grappling iron on to the edge of the boat.

A cry went up from the benches of the almadie. A movement of the waters brought the boat toward the stern of the ship with the velocity of an arrow. A monstrous wave pursued it even more rapidly.

"Come about!" cried Snorro. "To the oars, Brunhilde, to the oars!"

Scarcely had the vessel veered than the boat arrived, and the wave with it, curved over it like a funeral awning.

They were only a spear-length apart! They stretched out their hands to seize the liberating oars . . .

At the same instant, the menacing mountain inclined over their heads collapsed entirely . . .

The boat, those manning it, and three Danes who were holding out their oars had disappeared under the wave!

Two interlaced bodies were seen to reappear on the surface; a dying voice was heard to cry: "Save yourself, Siegmar, and let me perish!"

But that cry obtained no response, and the two lovers sank into the abyss again.

Snorro and his faithful followers had hurled themselves into the midst of the roaring waves. But when, after a long struggle against the waves, they rejoined their ship, they only brought two cadavers aboard.

They were those of Siegmar and the Jarl's daughter.

A PARTIAL LIST OF SNUGGLY BOOKS

G. ALBERT AURIER *Elsewhere and Other Stories*
CHARLES BARBARA *My Lunatic Asylum*
S. HEZOLNRY BERTHOUD *Misanthropic Tales*
LÉON BLOY *The Tarantulas' Parlor and Other Unkind Tales*
ÉLÉMIR BOURGES *The Twilight of the Gods*
CYRIEL BUYSSE *The Aunts*
JAMES CHAMPAGNE *Harlem Smoke*
FÉLICIEN CHAMPSAUR *The Latin Orgy*
BRENDAN CONNELL *Metrophilias*
BRENDAN CONNELL *Unofficial History of Pi Wei*
BRENDAN CONNELL (editor)
    The Zinzolin Book of Occult fiction
RAFAELA CONTRERAS *The Turquoise Ring and Other Stories*
DANIEL CORRICK (editor)
    Ghosts and Robbers: An Anthology of German Gothic Fiction
ADOLFO COUVE *When I Think of My Missing Head*
QUENTIN S. CRISP *Aiaigasa*
LUCIE DELARUE-MARDRUS *The Last Siren and Other Stories*
LADY DILKE *The Outcast Spirit and Other Stories*
CATHERINE DOUSTEYSSIER-KHOZE
    The Beauty of the Death Cap
ÉDOUARD DUJARDIN *Hauntings*
BERIT ELLINGSEN *Now We Can See the Moon*
ERCKMANN-CHATRIAN *A Malediction*
ALPHONSE ESQUIROS *The Enchanted Castle*
ENRIQUE GÓMEZ CARRILLO *Sentimental Stories*
DELPHI FABRICE *Flowers of Ether*
DELPHI FABRICE *The Red Sorcerer*
DELPHI FABRICE *The Red Spider*
BENJAMIN GASTINEAU *The Reign of Satan*
EDMOND AND JULES DE GONCOURT *Manette Salomon*
REMY DE GOURMONT *From a Faraway Land*
REMY DE GOURMONT *Morose Vignettes*
GUIDO GOZZANO *Alcina and Other Stories*
GUSTAVE GUICHES *The Modesty of Sodom*
EDWARD HERON-ALLEN *The Complete Shorter Fiction*
EDWARD HERON-ALLEN *Three Ghost-Written Novels*

J.-K. HUYSMANS *The Crowds of Lourdes*
J.-K. HUYSMANS *Knapsacks*
COLIN INSOLE *Valerie and Other Stories*
JUSTIN ISIS *Pleasant Tales II*
JULES JANIN *The Dead Donkey and the Guillotined Woman*
GUSTAVE KAHN *The Mad King*
MARIE KRYSINSKA *The Path of Amour*
BERNARD LAZARE *The Mirror of Legends*
BERNARD LAZARE *The Torch-Bearers*
MAURICE LEVEL *The Shadow*
JEAN LORRAIN *Errant Vice*
JEAN LORRAIN *Fards and Poisons*
JEAN LORRAIN *Masks in the Tapestry*
JEAN LORRAIN *Monsieur de Bougrelon and Other Stories*
GEORGES DE LYS *An Idyll in Sodom*
GEORGES DE LYS *Penthesilea*
ARTHUR MACHEN *N*
ARTHUR MACHEN *Ornaments in Jade*
CAMILLE MAUCLAIR *The Frail Soul and Other Stories*
CATULLE MENDÈS *Bluebirds*
CATULLE MENDÈS *Mephistophela*
ÉPHRAÏM MIKHAËL *Halyartes and Other Poems in Prose*
LUIS DE MIRANDA *Who Killed the Poet?*
OCTAVE MIRBEAU *The 628-E8*
CHARLES MORICE *Babels, Balloons and Innocent Eyes*
GABRIEL MOUREY *Monada*
DAMIAN MURPHY *Daughters of Apostasy*
KRISTINE ONG MUSLIM *Butterfly Dream*
OSSIT *Ilse*
CHARLES NODIER *Outlaws and Sorrows*
HERSH DOVID NOMBERG *A Cheerful Soul and Other Stories*
PHILOTHÉE O'NEDDY *The Enchanted Ring*
GEORGES DE PEYREBRUNE *A Decadent Woman*
HÉLÈNE PICARD *Sabbat*
JEAN PRINTEMPS *Whimsical Tales*
JEREMY REED *When a Girl Loves a Girl*
ADOLPHE RETTÉ *Misty Thule*
JEAN RICHEPIN *The Bull-Man and the Grasshopper*
FREDERICK ROLFE (Baron Corvo) *Amico di Sandro*

www.ingramcontent.com/pod-product-compliance
Lightning Source LLC
Chambersburg PA
CBHW020153120726
47903CB00007B/2544